I0684427

A Cowboy in Disguise

A Cowboy in Disguise

Victoria Ashe

Black Lyon Publishing, LLC

A COWBOY IN DISGUISE
Copyright © 2012 by Victoria Ashe

Our books may be ordered through your local bookstore or by visiting the publisher:

BlackLyonPublishing.com

Black Lyon Publishing, LLC
PO Box 567
Baker City, OR 97814

This is a work of fiction. All of the characters, names, events, organizations and conversations in this novel are either the products of the author's vivid imagination or are used in a fictitious way for the purposes of this story.

ISBN-10:   1-934912-51-4
ISBN-13:   978-1-934912-51-5
Library of Congress Control Number: 2012955527

Written, published and printed in
the United States of America.

Black Lyon Contemporary Romance

For God.
I'm grateful for every day.

Chapter One

"I don't care if he is the new executive flavor of the month. Just because he has the word 'senior' in front of his VP title doesn't make him qualified to lead this project." Alexandra Hunter leaned back in her seat and took a breath.

David stared at the woman who had been his vice president of marketing for the past three years. He looked for a brief second as if he wanted to run for the door. She narrowed her green eyes in determination and waited.

"Now look, Alexandra. I know you've brought this almost all the way to completion." David inhaled sharply and kept a conciliatory tone. Alexandra was too valuable to the firm and too good a friend for him to not understand where she was coming from—at least, that's what she hoped he thought.

Alexandra leaned forward in her chair again and uncrossed her long legs. "Exactly why *I* should be the one to see it all the way through the final presentation."

David sighed. "He knows the client personally, Alex. It's a surer sell."

Alexandra tucked a wayward strand of auburn hair behind her ear. "What you're proposing," she said coolly, "is to move the new guy in at the last minute and let him take credit for something I've worked on for over six months."

"As president, I'm looking out for your interests just as much as his. But the company's interests come first and that's why the two of you will be working together, and—" David raised his hand as Alexandra started to speak. "And that's why you'll present your proposal together as a team to the client." He had more gray hair at his temples than a month ago, she noticed.

"You mean the two of us working together?" Her voice remained calm. "David, if I didn't admire you so much, I'd quit right now."

"And if you weren't such a good employee, I might let you." He winked as she gave a dry smile and shut the door behind her.

She silently cursed him. He knew she wouldn't quit.

Alexandra's heels clicked loudly on the tiled floor all the way back to her office. If David thought some new glory-stealing, project-swiping pain-in-a-suit was going to take credit for her work, he had another thing coming.

"Sarah, come into my office for a sec," she called out as she turned the corner. "I'm going to need an extra set of everything I've put together for the Rio Safari presentation so far. Slide notes, the final proposal that made the shortlist—everything in the file. You won't believe what just happened."

Sarah shut the door. "Does it have anything to do with Scott Falconer?"

Alexandra dropped into her chair at the mention of her new nemesis' name and stared at her assistant. Was there ever any piece of information the woman didn't find out before everyone else in the building?

"How could you possibly know that?" she finally asked with all the calmness she could muster.

"Because he just called to say he'll be here tomorrow."

•

The next morning, Alexandra dressed carefully in an expensive gray silk suit and pulled her long hair back from her face, showing her high cheekbones to perfection. If she had to face the battle, she might as well do it in style. Alexandra Hunter knew she was known for her ability to remain calm and in control. If Falconer thought he could force her out of her own project or so much as get the pleasure of a reaction from her, he had another thing coming.

Her plan of attack would be what it always was, she thought as she pulled her car out of the driveway. She'd stay sensible and do her job wonderfully. Professional to the umpteenth degree. Give Falconer enough rope, and he would either prove himself useless twirling it about—or hang himself with it.

"Either way, he won't last long enough to give the presentation," she said aloud. "I'm sure of it."

She smiled to herself, a smile that quickly faded as the front of her car began to bounce roughly on the pavement. She looked into her side mirror, grimaced and muttered a few words she wouldn't want anyone to overhear.

"Great. Just what I need—in the middle of morning rush hour." Did she even have a spare tire with her? She couldn't remember. In fact, she didn't think she'd ever had to change a tire on this car.

Alexandra pulled the car over to the side of the busy Seattle freeway and took out her cell phone as she stood surveying the damage. A nail stuck out menacingly from the side of the tire. With a sigh, she gave a strong tug and jerked it free from the dirty, black rubber. The rest of the air hissed out in a rush as the car sank closer to the ground.

Then another ominous thought struck. There was no way she could change the flat without a jack, and she'd seen hers collecting dust in the corner of the garage just last week. She kicked the flat tire and yelped as her toe hit something hard. She'd miss her staff meeting and even worse, Falconer might make it to the office before she could limp in. She almost wished for a swift case of the flu to give her an excuse to call in sick. Was there any way for a person to call in dead?

Just as she started to dial, a shiny black BMW pulled off the road behind her. The driver turned off the engine and stepped from his car.

"Would you like some help?" he asked.

Alexandra stood spellbound as a striking man in an expensive, impeccably tailored suit approached. He walked with an air of control and social confidence she recognized from her own corporate training. He removed his sunglasses, revealing clear blue eyes that danced with energy as the wind blew his dark hair into them.

"I was just calling roadside assistance," she answered. She stood mesmerized as he took a few steps closer to her.

He shot her a wicked grin. "What am I? Roadkill?"

"Not from where I'm standing." Her hand flew to her mouth to stifle a laugh that took her by surprise. She turned off her cell phone, thankful the roar of the traffic had drowned out her voice.

The man took off his overcoat and jacket, and laid them gingerly over the hood. His white dress shirt clung to an athletic body. His tie was high quality silk, Alexandra noticed before shifting her gaze back to what was beneath the white dress shirt.

Wow.

"Was that a yes?" he asked when she didn't seem to intend to answer. "To the offer for help, I mean. Not to the equating me with roadkill part."

Alexandra quickly snapped out of her daze and smiled. "I don't have a jack with me." She was afraid she might actually be blushing. Her skin felt hot all the way down to her toes.

"Not a problem." He retrieved a jack from the trunk of his car and brandished it high. As he knelt beside the tire, Alexandra couldn't help but see the firm outline of his shoulder muscles as his shirt pulled tight across his broad back. His long fingers twirled the lug wrench around expertly. What was wrong with her? She forced herself to look away.

Alexandra felt the tiniest pang of regret when he finished. He all too quickly jumped to his feet and walked over. "All set."

He smiled brilliantly, seeming to hesitate for the slightest fraction of a moment. Alexandra was afraid he might simply wave and drive away without a word, so she tried to think of something to say that would stop him.

"Can I at least pay you?" she called out over the traffic noise. She was a corporate executive, adept at thinking on her feet, and this was the best she could come up with? Alexandra mentally kicked herself.

My brain has actually frozen.

Her rescuer took another step across the pavement and stood close enough for Alexandra to see tiny gray flecks in his robin-egg blue eyes. "No, you can't pay me," he answered. "It's enough that at least one person in the world will be happy with me today."

Alexandra held his gaze and was surprised at her own boldness when she said, "Well then, rest assured that I'm extremely happy at the moment." His bright, lopsided grin made her breath catch.

The man looked at his watch and grimaced. "I've never hated being responsible so much as at this very moment."

He reluctantly turned from her, grabbed up his expensive coat and drove away. In her stunned state, her fears had become real. The man had walked away and she didn't even know his name. And she'd been so consumed with the light-colored flecks in his eyes that she'd forgotten to ask after all.

"So much for introductions," Alexandra said aloud to herself and then sighed even louder in memory of those fantastic blue eyes ...

He was just the sort of man she'd love to date—if she could ever find the time or the trust. Tall, athletic, graceful and well-spoken. Her pulse had skipped a little just from looking at him, and she didn't even have a pulse she'd thought capable of skipping.

It had been months since her friends forced her to go out that last time, affectionately referred to as the "Date with the Living Dead."

Ever since then, she curled up in bed at night with budget spreadsheets and spent her days living with the thrill of closing the next deal. Besides, she'd worked too long and too hard to distract herself now. Not dating was safer—much, much safer. She had plenty of time for a social life—later. Maybe she should think about getting a cat, she mused. Then she could become the crazy cat lady and scare neighborhood children when she retired.

She smiled to herself. Then the smile faded. Sometimes she just felt tired all the way to the core.

Her Knight in Shining Sports Car nearly slipped from her mind as she pulled into the parking lot at the office. She looked up at the tall building looming in front of her and sighed, strangely wishing she was still stranded on the side of the road instead of steps from an encounter she wasn't going to enjoy. That building in front of her was the only world she knew, her means to an end.

She sighed again, remembering how the man's dark hair had waved across his forehead, giving him an almost boyish impression. And that smile—she couldn't shake the little feeling of butterflies it had created low in her stomach. It had been ages since she'd felt that feeling uncoil in her. She held on to the sensation until she stepped from the elevator and Sarah almost plowed her over.

"Where are you off to in such a hurry?" Alexandra asked.

The woman was nearly breathless. Were her hands actually shaking? "Grease remover. And antiseptic. Seeing if the cleaning staff has some. Back in a minute."

Alexandra watched her assistant scurry away. She could only guess what kind of tragic accident could have prompted the need for cleaner and peroxide. She just hoped the repair guys hadn't had another unfortunate incident with that copy machine on which they'd attached wheels. After that last runaway ...

Alexandra turned the corner to her office, and that's when she saw him—the man from the freeway sitting on the corner of her desk rubbing the front of his white dress shirt. The very sight of him stopped her dead in her tracks. *Oh no*, she thought, *this can't be*. The butterflies in her stomach fluttered mightily. This added a whole new and unneeded wrinkle to her desperate presentation-saving situation.

"Chivalry has its disadvantages," he said without looking up. The more he rubbed, the larger the black smear on the front of his shirt grew.

"So it seems."

Scott Falconer's gaze lifted slowly at the familiar sound of her voice. "Don't tell me you're Alex?"

She willed her feet to move again and stretched out her hand to shake his. "Alexandra. That would be me."

Scott laughed and took her hand in his warm, firm grasp. "Well, if this isn't ever fate."

"Something like that."

Alexandra's heart leapt into her throat and then landed firmly in the pit of her stomach. Great. Beautiful blue eyes on the devil himself. He was her enemy—the man poised to take away her presentation, her client and her authority. God had a sick, sick sense of humor, didn't He?

Her fingertips felt like fire in the palm of Scott Falconer's hand and she pulled away a little too quickly from the greeting.

"Still happy?" he asked quietly. His eyes sparkled.

Surely someone of his sort would continue to use that comment against her. Indefinitely. If he had any class or mercy in him at all, he'd let it drop. Before Alexandra could think of a cutting reply, Sarah returned empty-handed.

"Couldn't find a thing," the woman said. "Sorry. Oh, I did find a medical kit under the washroom sink for that knuckle. Do you have something to change into? You could at least put on a clean shirt."

He shrugged. "Not before a client meeting I have this morning, I'm afraid. Everything's at the hotel, so what I have on will just have to do. You know, I've found the freeways around here a lot friendlier than I'd thought," he said pointedly. "But alas, there's no time to drive back for a fresh shirt."

Had he really used the word "alas" out loud? She inhaled quietly. If Alexandra stayed annoyed or aloof enough, maybe the memory of her initial attraction to him would fade into oblivion. Besides, she could have sworn he was amused by her and that realization made her determined side come out all over again. She smiled brightly and forced herself to think something about bumbling idiots and enough rope.

"That's just too bad," she finally said in her most saccharine voice. "Maybe if you do up all the buttons on your jacket, it'll hide the spot."

Now where had *those* words come from? She certainly hadn't meant to be sarcastic either. Nothing came out right when she was near this man.

•

Scott shot her a questioning look. David had warned him this might be a rough transition and he'd really have to prove himself to win over the likes of Alexandra Hunter. But he wasn't sure if this situation was what he'd expected.

She was obviously annoyed with the entire scenario and exasperated with his mere existence, but all Scott could think about was how classically stunning she looked in the usually unflattering fluorescent office lighting. Beauty and competence fairly flew off of her in sparks.

He imagined the woman from the roadside in a thousand ways during the rest of his drive to the office. How might things have gone at this introduction they were now having, had he leaned in and kissed her tempting lips right there on the freeway? How would she have reacted had he pulled her into his arms and looked deeply into her emerald eyes?

A man could search all his life for a woman with her poise, her presence, and never find her. Yet Scott had been so shaken by his physical reaction to her that he'd panicked and walked away without so much as an introduction.

Now he was glad he hadn't acted on his impulses. The business gods were looking out for him.

"I don't think we did, but did we get off on the wrong foot somehow?" he asked quietly.

"Whatever gave you that idea?" she countered politely. "You were kind enough to change my tire. Thank you again for that."

He studied the stoic expression on her face for a moment. Stubborn.

"Well, in any case," he said, "I'm off to my meeting. David told me where your favorite restaurant is, so meet you there at five for an early dinner? It would be great to start going over the presentation details as soon as possible."

"So looking forward to it," she accepted with just a trace of ice in her voice. Or maybe he'd only imagined the ice.

Scott shot her another curious look and a dazzling smile, then buttoned up his jacket—all the way to the top as she had suggested. He didn't know what insanity had just made him invite a hostile woman to dinner, but he'd have to remember to ask David about that restaurant and hope Alexandra Hunter really did have a favorite.

•

Alexandra knew Sarah was lurking just around the corner. Waiting. Ready to pounce.

"Did you see him—what I just saw?" Sarah strolled into Alexandra's office and leaned dreamily against the wall. "He's absolutely beautiful. All that thick, dark hair with those blue eyes—and that body. Gosh, it's no wonder they say he has a new girlfriend every month. No one could resist a guy like that."

Alexandra's heart did a little sideways twist and settled even deeper into her gut. "Probably not the most appropriate office topic of conversation to be having, Sarah."

"Don't you even want to hear who he's dated?"

"Nope."

"Sunny Chezdous."

Alexandra couldn't help herself. "That trashy movie star?"

"None other," Sarah whispered. "And before that, he was with that pop singer, Kristina somethingerother. And they say he even dated that princess—you know, the one who's always causing all the scandals."

Alexandra sunk her head deep into the back of her leather chair and groaned. Scott Falconer's reputation was progressing—or deteriorating—from bad to worse.

But Sarah's enthusiasm wasn't to be quelled. "I also heard he grew up in Boston and spent his summers in France. Jet-setting, yachting and all that. Most definitely old money. Want to know more?"

"Probably never had to work a day in his life, right?"

"I can find out," she offered with a gleam in her eye. There was nothing Sarah enjoyed better than a good gossip-gathering mission.

"No, that's all right. I have a feeling I'll find out soon enough for myself."

David wouldn't put up long with an employee who sacrificed job performance for personal decadence. Maybe she'd found Falconer's Achilles heel.

Chapter Two

Just before five o'clock, Alexandra slipped out of her silk suit and into the simple black dinner dress she kept hanging on the back of her office door. She kept a pair of strappy black high-heeled shoes in her bottom desk drawer. If this old-money-playboy-exec-wannabe couldn't keep his head on straight in the company of beautiful, dumb women, she wondered how flustered he might get with an average-looking, smart one.

She couldn't remember wondering how a man might react since Duncan Phelps—and she'd nearly married that idiot.

She'd first met Duncan at a public relations seminar in New Orleans. He was working for a competitor at the time, but when he sauntered over to her table with his sandy blond hair and cocky grin, how could she have refused him? After all, people from several prominent companies mixed and mingled during these seminars.

Duncan had nearly made her pulse skip at first, too, she remembered, her thoughts sliding back to Scott for a moment. And there had been the surreal atmosphere of autumn in New Orleans, the romantic strolls down cobblestone walkways. Theirs had seemed the perfect start to a new relationship.

Alexandra's eyes misted over, purely from the infuriation she still felt with herself, and she quickly checked her mascara in the rearview mirror as she drove. Yes, theirs had been the perfect beginning, but what she'd never forget was the last evening she'd seen Duncan. The ending to beat all endings.

After work, she'd stopped and picked up Japanese takeout to bring over to his condo. She'd smiled all the way there just knowing they'd finally set a wedding date and found the right church for the ceremony. She'd been excited about shopping for a dress and having the invitations designed. Things couldn't have been better—or so she'd believed.

She hadn't recognized the red sports car in Duncan's reserved parking space, but she'd burst in through the front door without giving it much thought. Maybe he had a company car for the day. It didn't matter. She was just happy with the thought of seeing him again as she shut the door behind her.

Then her entire world went dark. All she could see was Duncan's face as he twisted around to look at her from a blanket spread out on the floor between the coffee table and the living room fireplace. As he pulled the blanket around himself and tossed another to the curvy little brunette beside him, Alexandra had hurled the takeout food at his head. The man was lucky she hadn't picked up pizza. A flatter box would have sailed faster toward his stupid face. She wondered if her aim had been good, and hoped it had—but she'd never looked back to check.

It wasn't until the next morning when she finally noticed her day planner and confidential client files were missing. In fact, everything to which Duncan had access was missing.

She'd never spoken to the man since, and the lawyers had discretely handled the low-profile corporate espionage case against him and his employers while she buried herself in work. Not so many months later, she accepted David's offer and left that tainted part of her career behind.

Alexandra shook off the bitter memories and finished wiping away a final streak of mascara. "That's what happens when you listen to your heart and not your head," she whispered to herself as she turned off her car's engine.

She locked the car door behind her and started to walk across the parking lot of her "favorite restaurant." The car in front from her looked awfully familiar. Could it be? It was. Scott's black BMW with both of its front tires completely flat, sitting sort of sideways in front of a spike strip.

"Should I even ask how you managed to do this?" Alexandra gestured toward the mutilated tires.

Scott looked up at her from on bended knee beside his fender. His eyes roamed her body for only a split-second, but she saw it, turned her head aside and grinned in spite of herself.

"Don't say another word." He laughed with a twinkle in his blue eyes. Steam rose up from the dark pavement behind him, a reminder it had rained only recently.

Alexandra bit her lip to keep from laughing outright. "I had no idea a flat was a contagious condition. And two of them? Guess that must qualify for an epidemic."

"Was that actually a smile?" He switched to his best phony southern accent. "Why ma'am, I do believe you're enjoying my suffering. But if that's what it takes to get a smile, I'll suffer gladly."

Suffer? Insufferable cad was more like it, she forced herself to think. When standing so near him, it was hard to remember she disliked everything this philandering glory-boy stood for.

"Can we eat now?" she said amicably. "I'm suddenly famished."

As they walked into the restaurant, the manager recognized Alexandra at once and greeted her warmly. They were escorted to the ideal table, far to the back of the room with very little lighting to show off the grease-stained front of his formerly white dress shirt and now-torn jacket. From the critical look he'd received, Scott suspected the restaurant manager would have hidden him at a grungy table near the kitchen or in front of the restroom doors if he hadn't seen Alexandra at his side.

"Please tell me dinner will be easier than the rest of the day was," Scott said with a little laugh.

Alexandra noticed his tired and yet still smiling face, and wondered if his patience ever ran thin. Maybe with the life of leisure he'd led, he never took anything seriously. He'd been pretty beaten up by the day, but the stress didn't seem to get to him the way it did to her. She thought to ask him how he'd liked his first day in her office, and then thought better of it.

After looking at him, she had to harden her heart and fast or they'd wind up sliding into small talk, which was a far too personal possibility considering their encounter that morning on the side of the road. Already she was having a hard time not staring into the depths of his eyes in the seductive candlelight. It was no wonder he was so adept at the playboy lifestyle. He came naturally equipped.

"We have a lot of information to go over, Mr. Falconer. I trust you've had a chance to read through my proposal?" Alexandra was suddenly more eager than ever to get down to business. If at all possible, she wanted to get through with the meal and the business discussion—immediately.

"Read it cover to cover," Scott answered. "We would never have made this shortlist if anyone else had written that submittal, you know. You intuitively knew just how to give that client what it needed. That's rare."

Alexandra was taken aback by the compliment and hoped it didn't show on her face. She cursed herself for being so susceptible to a kind word. She wasn't usually, but the compliment had seemed so genuine and personal coming from him. And from his confident tone, she might actually be fooled into believing he knew something about business after all. After talking with Sarah, she'd imagined he hadn't closed a deal on his own in his life.

"Well, I'm glad you agree with my approach," she finally said. "It should make pulling together the presentation that much easier." She spoke with a higher degree of aloofness than she felt, and politely took another bite of salad.

•

Scott sat back and chewed thoughtfully on a bread stick. The lady sure didn't know how to take a compliment with any warmth. He'd changed her flat tire, done serious damage to his wardrobe and his reputation as a sharp dresser, was thrilled when she turned out to be Alex—hell, he'd even paid her a professional compliment, which he never ever did unless it came highly deserved. And here she sat, treating him as if he made her smooth, creamy skin crawl.

"Look," he soothed. "I know this project is your baby, okay? And believe me, I know how a good executive feels about a project like that. But, here's the deal, Alex—"

"Alexandra," she corrected and then grimaced immediately as if she wished she hadn't. Their conversation was strained enough as it was.

"Fine. Alexandra. Rio Safari International has narrowed the shortlist down to three firms, including ours. Your proposal got us where we are. There's no doubt about that. But, the other two firms have done work for Rio in the past and you know one of them has a CEO who's married to the niece of some Rio VP or something like that. The other firm's CFO goes golfing every other Saturday with Rio's COO."

"But, David says you also have a personal connection. Seems we might need it." Alexandra smiled coolly at him. "So what exactly is your useful connection anyway?"

"I have several. Unfortunately, I also know the CEO."

"Ha!" Alexandra gloated. "So we have them trumped. At least as far as hierarchy goes."

He knew what she was thinking. That maybe his presence really did have merit after all. That she'd have to wait and hope he really could bring something to the table other than just a huge helping of glory hog.

"Let's hope."

Scott smiled back at her, wondering if her sudden cordial attitude was a setup for her next verbal sting. Either way, he sure wasn't going to let on exactly how he had come to know Rio Safari's CEO, Mac Stevens or how tenuous that situation might be. That story was too far in his past to dig up now, and somehow Scott cared what Alexandra thought and how she might judge him by his past ties.

Alexandra slid an outline in front of him. "I've started drafting up an approach for the presentation. Here, take a look at it. It's something to start with at least. They're giving us forty-five minutes to speak and another forty-five for Q&A at the end." She calmly took a sip of coffee, but the excitement of the deal was all over her expression. "Oh, and I've already warned the graphics department that we'll need at least a week fully dedicated. You know, poster boards, animations and all that. We'll blow their socks off."

Scott laughed out loud. That wall of ice she'd placed between them had finally melted away, he thought. "You're way ahead of me. And here I just wanted to get familiar with you and the office this week and hit the ground running next week. What was I thinking sleeping on the job like that?" He laughed again.

"Well, we've only got three weeks to pull this thing together. It'll be tight—" A small vertical stress line appeared above Alexandra's nose as she watched the look of surprise he knew must be plastered across his face. She had the look of someone who sensed bad news coming.

"I'm sorry, Alex. David must not have found time to tell you before you left the office. They've bumped the presentation date back two weeks. You and I have a trip to Colorado next week. Rio is asking all three competitors to come there for a little skiing at their private lodge. You know it's just political schmoozing, though. A chance to see who they like better." Scott saw that ice wall spring up again before he'd even finished his sentence.

"Well then, I suppose I'd better ask Sarah to make our travel arrangements, hadn't I, Mr. Falconer?"

•

Alexandra bit down hard on her fork.

How could David have kept this information from her? She should have been the next to know. It was only right. But instead the new guy was privy to information before she was, and she herself had written the proposal! Humiliating is what it was. She could feel the position of prestige she'd fought for start to slip away and suddenly her dinner salad turned over in her stomach. How could she have begun to like this man ... even a little?

Alexandra's darkening mood was apparently not lost on Scott. "I think I'd better get back to my hotel," he said with excellent timing. "And pray I have another shirt."

Scott paid for the dinner and handed Alexandra her coat.

"I'll get the expense code for this project for you. I hope you put our dinners on the company credit card," Alexandra said.

"Most definitely. I'm all business." He gave Alexandra what he probably hoped was his most winsome grin.

Alexandra grimaced at his comment as she pushed open the restaurant door. They walked without speaking to the parking lot. What more could she possibly have to say to Scott Falconer? All she wanted to do was go home and forget about the day. But as they reached the parking lot, they were just in time to notice a set of flashing amber lights far off down the street in front of them. As they watched, a rumbling tow truck disappeared around the corner with Scott's car rolling helplessly behind.

"I'm almost glad it was a rental, considering the day it's seen. I miss my pickup." He sounded truly weary for the first time. "Think Sarah can work her magic and get the car out of impound tomorrow? And maybe even return it to the rental place for me?"

"Sure."

Alexandra felt the impulse to be kind rush through her in spite of her frustration. Calm, collected Alexandra Hunter—and here she was with her emotions on a roller coaster just because of a man. One minute she wanted to dislike him and thought she might. The next minute his gaze sent tingles racing through her. Maybe she should make him walk? Or call a taxi for him?

"Hop in. I'll give you a ride."

"I was hoping you'd ask," he said with a sigh. "I really didn't feel like waiting for a cab."

As they drove along, Scott watched the stars out the passenger window. "It's beautiful tonight. Not as beautiful or clear as the sky where I grew up, though."

"Boston or Paris?"

He turned away from the window and laughed so hard he almost choked. "Try Montana."

"Montana?" Alexandra shot back at him. She knew her face

flushed red. Sarah was going to be in so much trouble when she got hold of her ... Then Alexandra glanced over at Scott and saw the start of a five o'clock shadow, a gaping hole in his jacket sleeve, and black goo smeared up and down the entire front of his shirt. Two of his knuckles were scraped and bloody from one tire-changing incident or another, and a chunk of dark brown hair sprouted up awkwardly from his head like a weird antenna.

"Now you're laughing at me?" Scott asked in amazement. "I'll have you know that Montana is a very nice place to be raised."

Alexandra wiped her eyes with the back of her hand. "No, no. It's not that at all. I think you should look in the mirror, Mr. Falconer. You're a complete mess." He certainly was hard to hate.

"I can't bear to look at myself," Scott said while he watched her long legs move to work the pedals as the hem of her dress crept up higher on her thighs.

She was aware of where his gaze went. She knew her eyes looked softer in the faded light and her black dress shifted over a figure he had to know he shouldn't be noticing in a business colleague. She wasn't oblivious.

"You should also know," she continued, "that your reputation has far outdone you." If he wasn't the jet-setting type, she suspected everything else Sarah had said was false, too. Listening to gossip should have been beneath her—just one of the many imperfections she was trying to work on.

"Is that a good thing or are you disappointed?" he asked.

"Well, I'd say it's definitely a good thing. Rumors of your reputation aren't exactly anything I'd want to live up to. I hear you've kept company with questionable royalty and assorted celebrities. You've had quite the obscene life of privilege and leisure—what with all that flitting back and forth between Paris and Boston." She shot him an amused look. "I think I'll have to let you know what else I hear along the way."

"You know, I think I've heard that rumor about a princess in Paris or something. Never happened. I was raised in Montana, worked my way through college and worked some more to get here. That's about all. Pretty uneventful. I'm just your average cowboy."

Alexandra snorted at his description of himself. The last thing she would call this particular senior vice president was a cowboy. She laughed again and imagined him rounding up cattle on horseback wearing one of his expensive suits, his briefcase hanging over the saddle.

"So you've worked in the industry for a while?" She really was curious now.

"Ever since I graduated from the university. I majored in business and finance, but somehow it got parlayed into a marketing career over the years."

"I know how that tends to happen."

She was pretty sure Scott wasn't sure how to read her after she quit talking. After all, one minute she was cutting him down to the quick with excessive politeness, and the next she'd gone all soft on him. She'd actually laughed.

He apparently decided to venture out on a limb.

"Alex, look," he said in a gentle tone. "I'm sorry for whatever it was I did wrong. We obviously got off to a bad start somehow, but I really admire your work and I really, really don't have any designs on your position or your project."

Alexandra stopped the car in front of his hotel. "No, I'm the one who should be sorry. I can get too protective of my work, and after all I'd heard about you, I just thought—"

"That I was horning in on your territory?" he finished.

"Exactly," she conceded.

"Why is this project so important to you? I've seen dedication, but not like this."

She paused and looked straight ahead. "It's all I have."

"What do you mean?"

"I have food to put on the table and bills to pay just like everyone else. Except in my case, there's no one to fall back on if I fail."

"What about your parents?"

"No longer living." She brushed a strand of hair out of her eyes. "But enough of that."

She waited to see if he'd pry or not. Seconds ticked by.

"So what do you think now? Friends?" he asked at length.

"Oh, friendly colleagues at the very least." She smiled. "Good night, Scott."

She saw it in his eyes—he hadn't missed that she'd finally called him by his first name and he liked it. And neither of them missed the connection in their gaze that lasted just a heartbeat longer than necessary.

"'Night, Alex."

Chapter Three

"So, let me get this straight. You've been partnered up with a guy who's gorgeous, smart, funny, sensitive, has a great career—and you *don't* want to go to Colorado with him? Are you nuts?" asked Mary, chief instigator of the Date with the Living Dead.

Alexandra paused for a moment, not sure how to answer her friend on the other end of the phone. Mary always had a way of filtering out everything important, she thought. Just listen to her. She'd fixated on the one mention of Scott and ignored everything else Alexandra had just tried to tell her.

She sighed. "Leave it to you to turn the situation into a romantic intrigue. It's just that I hadn't planned on going away next week. It's not that I don't want to go."

"So then you do want to go with him?"

Alexandra rolled a soft sound of frustration around in her throat. "We'll lose the client if I don't."

"You actually like this guy," Mary squealed into the phone. "That's what it is. I can't believe it."

"I just don't dislike him the way I thought I would. Ever since Duncan—"

"Ugh. Duncan again. For the last time, nobody is like Duncan," Mary interjected. "The odds of you ever meeting someone that slimy again are ten million to one. Probably more. When they made him, the mold cracked itself in half just to get away from him."

Alexandra couldn't help but laugh. "I know. I know. But, I

really thought Scott was coming here to take over my project and push me aside. Then I believed all these rumors about him. I really haven't treated the guy very well." Alexandra slapped her palm against her forehead, realizing she was about to let Mary draw her into yet another discussion about her love life. "Hey, Mary," Alexandra continued, "I've got to get to the airport."

"Way to change the subject, Ms. Alexandra. I'll be waiting for an update when you get back. I have the feeling this is going to be one heck of a trip."

Alexandra set the receiver back down on the phone. One heck of a trip? She didn't know whether to dread it or look forward to it.

Lost in thought, she arrived at the airport before she knew it.

Alexandra had the window seat. She always liked to watch the buildings shrink away beneath her as the massive silver plane climbed in the sky. But now she was looking forward across all the seats before hers, watching the front of the plane in anticipation and searching the boarding passengers for a familiar face. Where was he? All she could see was a jumble of strange faces and their carry-on luggage.

At last she spotted Scott in the crowd. Freshly showered and impeccably dressed, the contrast between the Scott with whom she'd had dinner and this Scott was incredible. She'd nearly forgotten how striking he'd looked to her that first moment he stepped out of his BMW on the freeway.

He wore a gray sweater that somehow transformed the blue of his eyes to cobalt. Loose-fitting jeans flowed from his narrow hips down across long, muscular legs, all the way to a pair of polished black cowboy boots. Alexandra was glad Mary wasn't there to see her expression as Scott shoved his baggage underneath the seat and sat beside her. In such close quarters, it was impossible for her not to catch the scent of him—a mix of dryer sheets, mild shaving gel and the naturally warm smell of his skin.

Oh, she was in trouble.

•

"'Mornin', Sunshine," he quipped as he settled into his seat. He tried not to look at her too directly. The top two buttons of her forest green blouse were undone, revealing just a hint of her curves. She was stunning in the soft golden light that came with the sunrise.

"Sleep well?" she asked.

"Great," he lied.

In the middle of the night he had woken with a start from a dream so intense he feared he might blush if he met Alexandra's eyes now. He hadn't gotten back to sleep again before his four o'clock AM wake-up call started him on his way to the airport.

"Figures. I get here last, I get stuck with the middle seat," he said. An enormous man squeezed into the aisle seat beside him, forcing him even physically closer to Alexandra.

"How much will you offer for the window seat?" she teased.

He gave a low whistle. "Mercenary to the core."

He grinned wickedly, all lightness and liveliness. For someone who hadn't slept, he felt strangely energetic all of the sudden.

"Look, there goes our office complex," Alexandra pointed out as the plane lifted higher and higher. "And the Space Needle is way, way over there."

Scott leaned over her to peer out the window. "Seemed even farther from the airport when I was driving for some reason."

Alexandra turned her head away from the window to speak and found herself cheek to cheek with him. She looked as if all the blood in her body had just rushed to her face.

Scott leaned slowly back, realizing how dangerously close his lips were to hers, how their arms touched side to side on the armrest. "I'm sorry," he whispered. "I think I invaded your space." A whiff of the lightly exotic perfume oil she so enjoyed wearing filled his senses.

He watched Alexandra dig her long nails into her palms. She acted as if she had her whole world to lose just by liking him. It was a cardinal rule of business—never, ever become romantically involved with a co-worker. Somehow the man always outranked the woman, and somehow the woman was always the one to lose her job when the relationship soured. He'd seen it happen. But, he hadn't made an overture at all, had he?

After a long pause she said, "I picked up the agenda for our Colorado adventure on the way here." She handed him a copy, too careful not to touch his hand as she started to read down through the document.

Scott paraphrased, "Looks like we just get to hang out with the competition for the first night. Says that the next day each of the competing firms moves from a hotel up to individual cabins farther up in the mountains."

"What was that?" Alexandra gripped the papers tightly. "That can't be right. We were all supposed to be staying in Rio Safari's private lodge." She scanned frantically for more information. "Oh. Their waterline apparently froze and burst. The lodge is closed up tight."

Scott read the guest roster. "You're the only female on this list. They have you down as Alex Hunter, so I'm pretty sure some misguided travel agent didn't realize."

"That I'm a woman?" She chewed her lower lip. "I imagine these cabins have private bedrooms. We'll be sharing the common areas for sure, but I'm sure we'll be okay."

"Why wouldn't we be okay?" he asked with a smile. It was hard for him to imagine anyone might not realize Alexandra Hunter was a woman. He felt a thrill zap through his body as he noticed how nervous the usually poised lady seemed to be. Her fingers were literally crushing the papers she held.

"I mean I'm sure we'll have privacy enough," she said. "It's a little awkward for a man and a woman on a business trip to be sleeping together in such close quarters, don't you think?"

"You're right," he assured. "But I'm sure we'll be fine."

"Because you know," she added, "I'd hate to contribute any to your sterling reputation."

She gave him a playful eyebrow raise, reclaiming her composure as the flight attendant walked by selling cooled masks made of some type of gel meant to lull sleepy passengers back into dreamland. Considering his lack of sleep the night before, Scott bought two and handed one to Alexandra. With the glare blocked from their eyes, they were both dozing before they knew it. Only his nearness to Alexandra kept Scott from falling dead asleep.

He wondered if she was usually able to even nap on planes, wondered if just maybe she hadn't slept well the night before, either. Scenes from the day kept replaying themselves in his mind, and he just couldn't seem to turn off his thoughts.

He'd bet she rehearsed lines she'd say when she finally got to meet Rio's executive team. At one point she probably got up and reread her own proposal, as if she hadn't memorized it word for word long ago.

Scott stirred before Alexandra, just as the plane started to descend. He almost wished her head had fallen against his shoulder like he always saw happen in the movies. But, she stayed politely in her seat, smiling softly even in her sleep. A long wave of hair had fallen down across her face and clung to the corner of her lips. On impulse, Scott reached across and gently pulled the strands back away from her face. Her hair felt like silk against his fingertips.

"What are you doing?" she asked calmly with her eyes still closed.

"I didn't want you to eat your own hair," he whispered. "I hear it doesn't make for the most nutritious breakfast."

"Such a thoughtful gentleman."

She stretched with her arms high above her head, and he looked away quickly as the fabric of her shirt shifted subtly, almost seductively with the motion.

"Ready to intimidate the competition?" he asked. What was with him anyway? If he didn't know better, he thought he just might start blushing himself.

"You bet."

He'd never been so relieved or so disappointed to get off an airplane in his life, but good news greeted them at the reception desk. Having only just arrived, their odds had already improved. It seemed one of the other firms was conspicuously absent from the gathering. Its team, having been pulled away at the last minute to Houston, had sent a meager note of apology.

"You know what this means," Alexandra whispered to Scott.

"Oh, yes," he answered. "One down, one to go. Rio will let them give a presentation for legal procurement reasons, but they're as good as out of the running. Rio wants to be the priority, and if a company can't give that to them, then ..."

"Exactly," Alexandra agreed.

The desk clerk approached them. "Excuse me," she said. "Three gentlemen from Zellez Corporation have already arrived. They're waiting to meet you in the lounge."

"That's strange," Alexandra told Scott. "There were only two enemy names from Zellez on the invitee list."

"Maybe they're overcompensating," he only halfway kidded.

As they approached the lounge, all Scott and Alexandra could see at first were the backs of three men all dressed for winter, sipping coffee or hot chocolate in front of a roaring fire.

"Watch this," Alexandra whispered to Scott. Straightening her posture and smoothing the front of her tan slacks, she strode confidently into the lounge with Scott not missing a beat at her side.

Two of the men rose instantly to greet her, obviously in admiration of her looks, her professional reputation, or both. She absolutely filled the room with her presence as she and Scott shook hands with the men.

Just as quickly as the confidence had surfaced, horror replaced it in her expression. The third man set his drink down quietly and stood a step behind his companions with his thumbs tucked casually in his pockets.

The Alexandra Hunter he knew didn't choke under pressure. She certainly did not have attacks of shyness during introductions. Scott caught her look of panic immediately and extended his hand to the third man. "Scott Falconer, D. W. Songstram Corporation."

The man with the sandy blond hair reluctantly shook Scott's hand. "Duncan Phelps, vice president of business development and marketing, Zellez."

Scott fought the urge to wipe his hand off on his jeans. The man was dressed in a tweed jacket and had a closely trimmed goatee and mustache. His tan skin and white teeth were falsely bright and Scott thought he looked like the womanizing professor version of one of those plastic dress-up dolls.

"Duncan, I'd like to introduce our star executive, Ms. Alexandra Hunter. She's done wonders for the company as our vice president of marketing."

Duncan smiled and returned his thumbs to his pockets. "We've met."

Alexandra recovered herself. "Well, now there's a face I didn't expect to see here." Her voice was exceedingly cordial and without a trace of real warmth. "Duncan, gentlemen, it's been a pleasure. But unfortunately, I need to steal Mr. Falconer away to go over some boring details. You'll excuse us?"

With her head held high, she led Scott away down the hall. "Thank you for the save back there," she said as she fumbled with the key card to her room. Her face looked ghostly white and she breathed in one too many deep breaths to be normal.

Scott gently took the card from her shaking hand and held open the door for her. "That's what friendly colleagues are for."

Alexandra paced the room, and Scott wasn't sure if she wanted to laugh, cry or scream.

"Ohhh," she repeated a few times as she sat down on the edge of the bed and rubbed her temples with her fingers. "We have a big problem here."

"Who was that guy?"

"How in the world did he make vice president? Do you know how hard I worked to be the youngest VP in D. W. Songstram history? He's not much older than me and has half the accomplishments." Alexandra jumped up and paced the floor. "Shouldn't surprise me I guess. I'm sure his former employer gave glowing references. He did business just the sleazy way they liked it, after all."

"Alex, how do you know him?" Scott rephrased the question to get her attention.

She turned to him, anger igniting her eyes. "That lowlife stole a bunch of confidential documents from me and the last company I worked for. He took client lists, patent pending information—he even got my personal notes. Scott, I shouldn't even be telling you all this. I'm not supposed to say a word. The court order stipulated it."

"We have to find a way to inform Rio. The man's a felon."

"No, no he's not. Not technically anyway." She sat back down on the bed. "Their lawyers were eager to keep the whole thing quiet and out of the courts. Duncan's company agreed to return all of our property, terminate his employment immediately and pay a hefty settlement. In exchange, my company signed a gag order. Of course we'd have been able to testify in criminal court in spite of the gag, but the district attorney never looked at the case again. They felt there wasn't enough evidence to pursue criminal charges. What a crock."

"Had they bought off the D.A.?"

She nodded. "I always suspected so. Of course, we'll never really know, will we? All we can do is guess."

Scott ran his hand through his wavy hair. "So the gag order holds and we can't say a word."

"Not unless we want him to sue David's company and both of us personally."

Scott put his hand on her shoulder and squeezed it gently. "We're a stronger team than they are anyway. We'll win on our qualifications and that glorious proposal you put together, and no matter what Duncan Phelps does, it won't matter worth a darn anyway."

Alexandra breathed out the last of her stress and Scott was suddenly very aware that the two of them were sitting on her bed alone together in her room, and that he had his hand resting comfortably on her shoulder. It would be so simple to lean closer and …

"Don't worry, Alex. Schmucks like Duncan Phelps always get what's coming to them in the end."

"That's exactly what I've been telling myself for the last three years."

He pulled his hand away. "I'd better go see if my room looks as good as yours does."

He already knew it wouldn't even as he stepped into the hall. In fact, it couldn't look half as good—Alexandra wasn't in it.

Chapter Four

The next morning came soon and before they knew it, a snowcat driver was busy tossing their luggage into the cab of the vehicle. "Bet you folks are surprised to see this contraption. Most people expect a little fancier ride on their way up to the Rio Cabins."

"I thought we'd just take a truck or something. Are the roads really that bad?" Alexandra asked the driver as they started to bounce along ruts in the snow.

"Nah. They're fine for this time of year. The cabins are about six miles past the last plowed road so it's a little hard for anything else to make it up there."

"Can we ski or snowshoe back out?" Scott asked.

"It's a long way, but you could. Nobody's ever tried it I don't think. Have to be in darn good shape. Otherwise, I'll be back up in a couple days to bring you all back. I've got to make another trip in a bit to haul the guys from that other firm up here. Can't fit everyone in the snowcat at once. So now's the time to holler if you left anything at the hotel. Anyway, I think you'll have a good time," he continued. "Mac Stevens has a private ski lift and groomed slope up behind the cabins. You can cross-country ski or go snowmobiling if you want. It's a great place to get away."

Safe at the cabins, Scott and Alexandra watched the driver pull away and disappear in the distance. "Remember that horror movie where the family is supposed to spend the winter in the haunted hotel and the man goes nuts and tries to chop up his wife?" Alexandra asked with one long stream of breath.

"Yeah, so?"

"I'm pretty sure that hotel was just over those hills." She watched nervously as the last puff of exhaust from the snowcat evaporated far away down the road.

"Try to find a bright side."

The snow was deep and still falling rapidly. Alexandra shivered. "Well, at least I don't have to drive in this foul stuff."

"That's the spirit." Scott laughed and flung a lump of snow in her direction.

"Don't you dare, Falconer. I'll report you to the company president. I know him personally, you know."

They were still laughing as they opened the door to their cabin. The building was smaller than expected, but to Alexandra's relief, there were two separate bedrooms rather than just two beds in the middle of a larger room. She'd been right about the shared bathroom, though.

"No wi-fi for sure. I wonder if there's any internet access at all," she called out as she explored.

"Can't see any way there would be, and I doubt I'll find one. It doesn't even look like we have a TV in here. Got an old radio—not the music kind, though. CB or something. And a fireplace. Looks like there's food in the cabinets." He stopped exploring, curiosity satisfied. "There are down pillows and huge down comforters on both beds." He grinned. "I haven't curled up in one of those since I was a kid. Hope you're not allergic to feathers."

Alexandra was all business. "Knowing Duncan, I expected the Zellez team to beat us to the cabins. I'm surprised."

"Actually," Scott said, "I think I hear a motor right now. Maybe it's them. That was awfully fast, though. Think the snowcat moves that fast?"

They stepped outside and walked a few feet in the direction of the road, but in the near blizzard conditions, all they could see was white. The buzz of a motor echoed through the snowbanks.

Scott's dark eyebrows drew together. "Sounds more like a snowmobile than the snowcat. Who in the world would be out here now?"

A loud bang, muffled and amplified at the same time by the insulation of all that snow, startled them. Alexandra and Scott looked at each other, both knowing an explosion when they heard one. Two, three, then four more charges roared out in succession, and that's when they heard an even more menacing sound.

"Get in the cabin. Run!" Scott grabbed Alexandra's hand and pulled her with him.

The noise started low and then mixed with the crash and snap of breaking tree limbs. Alexandra ran behind Scott, nearly catching up to him until her foot caught on a piece of wood partially buried in the snow, and her legs twisted under her. She looked up to see a wall of pure white coming down at them.

Scott swept her up from the ground and bolted the cabin door behind them. They ran to the back bedroom, trying to get as far from the front of the cabin as possible. The rumble grew deafening as the avalanche collided with the cabin, shaking it like a small earthquake might.

When the noise subsided, they stood and walked into the living room. Though now blocked with snow, the front door had held up against the onslaught. Snow buried the front of the cabin up to the middle of its windows.

Alexandra looked out through a crack in the broken glass. "Looks like most of it headed straight down the roadway. Path of least resistance." She wondered if they might still have a chance of digging out. But even if they did, where would they go?

"I'll try to round up some help."

As Scott examined the radio, Alexandra walked back to her room to see if she might have anything in the way of entertainment in there. At least a book or two might help pass the time until someone came to dig them out, she thought.

Scott dusted the cobwebs off the old radio and called out for help. He reached the desk clerk back at the hotel, and she told him to wait while she looked for the snowcat driver who'd just made it back to the hotel. Scott listened to static come over the radio before the driver's voice finally broke through.

"You there?" the driver called out.

"I'm still here," Scott said.

"It's snowing like mad down here. Had a hard time getting back in the blizzard. Didn't think it'd hit us that hard."

"We've got an even bigger problem." The connection on the radio was breaking up.

"A problem? Did you say something about a problem?" The driver must have been yelling into his microphone.

"Yeah. We just about got buried in an avalanche. Can't even get the cabin door open yet."

"Avalanche?" the driver yelled back. "You two didn't get hurt, did you?'

"We're fine, but can you send some help? Someone to dig us out?"

There was nothing but static for several seconds. "I didn't quite catch that last part. Hang on a minute. I've gotta go check something out."

Scott waited for a couple minutes listening to the static. Hopefully the blizzard hadn't knocked out the weak signal altogether.

The snowcat driver came back to his microphone. "Bad news. Dang D.O.T. workers went and blasted by mistake. Set off a controlled avalanche on the wrong week. With the snow coming down the way it is, it was gonna be hard to haul those guys from the other company up to the cabins today anyway. 'Bout impossible now. Can't get you two back here either. Better just stay warm and safe inside. We'll call in tomorrow."

"You won't believe it," Scott announced as Alexandra came around the corner. "The driver says the transportation department made a mistake and set off a planned avalanche at the wrong time. They got their dates crossed and now we're stuck."

Alexandra's ankle had begun to swell a little. "As least finding ice won't be a problem," she joked.

"Looks like we'll just have to get comfortable and wait for someone to get us tomorrow."

Alexandra elevated her foot while Scott started a blaze in the big stone fireplace. Thankfully, the cabin was well-prepared for guests and had a large pile of dry wood inside. This was their good luck since they didn't have another source of heat or light. The avalanche had apparently knocked out the electricity somewhere along the line. The sensuous glow from the fire bathed the room, making it surprisingly warm and comfortable.

Alexandra hobbled over to the kitchen cabinets to take inventory. "Here we have aluminum foil and a few potatoes. I'll just wrap some up and toss them onto the coals—and voilà— dinner."

With her hair back in a thick ponytail and her oversized plaid shirt, she certainly didn't look or feel like a high-ranking executive at the moment. Of course, with Scott in his long underwear top and loose jeans, he didn't look much like one either, she realized.

"Alex," he chided, taking a potato out of her hand, "go put that ankle up on a stack of pillows or you won't be able to stand upright in those high heels of yours for weeks to come. Gym shoes don't go well with silk suits during a presentation."

"Suit yourself." She tossed him another potato and smiled when he caught it. "I'm not one to complain when a man offers to wait on me hand and foot." And a gorgeous one at that, she thought and then immediately tried to convince herself she hadn't.

Alexandra snuggled down on the wide couch and watched him heat up soup for her in the fire. She relaxed her head back into a fluffy pillow and moaned. Mary's voice came to her like the proverbial devil on her left shoulder, "The two of you, trapped alone together in a cabin—think of the possibilities." Alexandra groaned again.

Scott heard her and called out, "Are you in pain?"

"No, no, I'm fine."

The angel on her other shoulder chimed in, "Never get

involved with a co-worker. Your reputation will be destroyed."

"Dinner is served," he announced with a sweeping gesture across the little table.

Alexandra limped over to her chair. Scott had managed to pull together a meal of hot cream of chicken soup, crackers, beef jerky and semi-burnt baked potatoes. She suspected he didn't often visit his own kitchen, so this was a valiant effort.

They went over presentation strategies again until reading by firelight started to strain their eyes, and then Alexandra retired to her room. She was glad for the retreat to solitude. With every turn of the page, she had watched Scott's arm muscles play underneath the very masculine long underwear top he had on. More than once she'd had to look away in hopes he hadn't noticed her intense awareness of him.

She heard Scott stoke the fire once more and then walk back toward his own room. He stopped outside her bedroom door and panicked anticipation rushed through her. At last he turned away, but the situation was no better. He slept just on the other side of a single, thin wall. She ran her hand along the paneling and on a whim, knocked on it lightly with her knuckles. Her hand flew to her mouth in absolute horror.

Scott reappeared in the faint glow of the firelight coming in through her open door. "Everything okay?"

"Yes. Just hit the wall by accident," she called out, pulling the blankets up tighter under her chin. He looked amazing silhouetted in the doorway, tall and rugged as if he belonged in a cabin more than he ever could in an office. She wondered what he slept in at night and then pushed that thought quickly out of her head along with all the rest.

"Do you think you'll be able to sleep?" he asked with a deep, quiet voice that carried to her through the near darkness. He hadn't moved from the doorway.

"Not if you keep standing there talking to me," she answered. Heaven help her, even his voice was sexy.

Scott's hand lingered on the doorframe. "If you object so much to me standing here, I can change that."

Was his voice huskier than usual? Could he actually be thinking of coming into her bedroom? Her emotions spun, but all that came out of her mouth was, "I was objecting to the talking part."

Now Alexandra could have slapped herself. She knew her phrasing had opened her up wide for a lowbrow innuendo something to the effect of, "Well, baby, who said we needed to talk."

But Scott didn't sink to the occasion. "Good night, Alex."

His silhouette left the doorway and Alexandra soon heard him snuggle under his own down comforter as the bed frame creaked under his weight. She felt a pang of regret even though she convinced herself she had no real reason to. Someday. Yes, maybe someday she could come back to a cabin like this with a husband and children. Someday when there was more to life than work. Down comforters just weren't meant to snuggle up in alone. Once again, she was tired all the way to the core.

•

Alexandra hobbled into the living room the next morning to find Scott already up and digging around the cabinets, already thinking of breakfast. She noticed he'd showered, but had apparently decided not to shave—and it suited him. There wasn't much that didn't suit him—even stubble and long underwear.

"Mornin'," he called out. "I've got tea, canned peaches and oatmeal. Think you can choke that down?"

"Sounds great," she said as she eased herself onto a kitchen chair. "I'm going to get spoiled if I don't watch out."

"How's the ankle?"

"Better. Maybe a little more purple, but I'll definitely live through it."

He finished putting food in front of her. "I radioed down to the hotel earlier this morning. We're stuck up here at least another day. They're not plowing until tomorrow at the soonest."

"I think we can dig out the front door today. Most of the snow is along the side of cabin and the blizzard stopped, so I'll bet we can get it open."

"It would be great to get outside into the fresh air again." He flashed her a dazzling smile, teeth looking whiter than usual against his dark new stubble.

Alexandra had been right—they could dig out. After breakfast, they put on their gloves and were slowly able to shove away the snow blocking the door until they could push it open just wide enough to slip through. To one side of the cabin and down the road, a bank of snow several feet high stood as testimony to the avalanche from the day before. But on the other side, the snow was shallow enough that they could trudge through it.

"What if Zellez is using this time to seal the deal?" she asked once they were outside.

"It's beyond our control."

The sun was bright in a clear blue sky and the trees on the mountains stood still without a breeze when Alexandra and Scott finally squeezed through the door. The day was glorious with the sunlight bouncing off flawless hills of snow, lighting them up like a million tiny diamonds.

"Just think," he said, "there's no one around for miles and all of this is ours for a day." Scott stood with his hands on his hips looking up at the mountains. He wore a thick black ski jacket with blue piping and a heavy pair of boots coordinated to match the jacket. He had definitely packed for the location better than Alexandra had thought to.

"It may be all ours, but what do we do with it?" Alexandra peered out from inside the fur-lined hood of her white coat. A snowflake or two settled onto her long lashes and melted. She breathed in deeply of the clean air and started to say something else to Scott.

From out of nowhere, a lump of snow hit her on the side of the head. "Hey!" she yelled, "no fair." She bent down to pack a snowball of her own when another struck her on the backside. "This is war," she declared. Alexandra hurled a well-packed ball at Scott, hitting him squarely in the chest.

"You throw like a girl," he taunted as he threw another

snowball at her and missed.

"Oh yeah? At least I have the excuse of actually being a girl—unlike some people I know." She let two more snowballs sail and watched with great satisfaction as one struck Scott on top of his head and disintegrated into powder, some of which slid down into the neck of his coat.

Scott jumped around trying to shake the freezing snow out of his coat before it melted down his back. "Time out," he pleaded as another snowball pelted him the face.

Alexandra put her hand over her mouth and hobbled quickly over to him. "Are you all right?"

As she examined him, he swung around with a hidden handful of the white stuff and smeared it solidly in Alexandra's face.

"Rat," she started to say and pushed him playfully in the chest with one hand as she wiped the snow away with the other. But her push didn't move Scott—it only served to propel her own body backward on the slick surface, and with her already injured ankle, she began to lose balance.

As if in slow motion, her feet started to go out from under her. Scott reached out to steady her, but his own feet slid away from him as she grabbed onto his arm and pulled him down with her into the snow.

Alexandra's hood had fallen back from her face and her skin was rosy from the cold. Her auburn hair flowed freely, framing her face in damp waves. Her pants were miserably soaked through with melting snow, and when Scott sat up in the snow beside her, she noticed his were, too.

"I win," Alexandra said.

"What do you mean? I got the last point."

"Point?" she countered. "If we're talking points here, I got more of them. You missed most of the time."

"You're a smaller target," he argued.

"You used sneak attacks."

Alexandra's voice trailed off as she suddenly realized how closely they were sitting together and how intensely Scott was watching her.

His gaze met hers and held it as he removed his gloves and gently brushed a lump of snow out of her damp hair. Slowly he leaned toward her, his lips perilously close to hers. Anticipation glittered in his eyes and Alex knew she must look the same as him.

Her lips, red from the cold, parted as her breath caught. He pressed his lips tentatively against hers in a sweet, soft kiss full of restraint as he waited for some sign of how she might react. Would she slap him? Yell at him? Sue him? She didn't even know.

This was truly forbidden. If anyone suspected two executives were fooling around, the rumors would tear their careers apart. She hadn't been able to concentrate on the presentation as it was—her thoughts had been saturated with Scott. If only she could push him away, tell him no, talk to him in that excessively polite way of hers.

Alexandra's breath caught as Scott's lips found hers. She felt a current pass between them, erasing all other sensations. She immediately missed the taste of his breath, sweet and warm, as his lips left hers.

Scott rested his forehead against hers. "This is a bad idea." He breathed. His lips brushed against hers as he spoke. "We shouldn't even start this."

Somewhere, his words reached her. This was no game. This was her career, her reputation, her livelihood on the line. Inspired by self-preservation, a fleeting memory of Duncan and her last bit of self-restraint, Alexandra quickly pulled away.

"You're right. I can't get involved with you. And you can't get involved with me." She stood and limped as fast as she could back inside the cabin.

They each retreated awkwardly to their rooms without another word. It had only been a kiss, Alexandra rationalized. That was all it was. Nothing for two adults to panic over. No damage done. Alexandra's senses slowly began to come back to her as the memory of his kiss faded from her lips.

She closed her eyes and relived his lips caressing hers so very briefly. She imagined each of strong features from his straight nose to his heavy eyebrows and back down to his square chin. She couldn't think of a single thing she would change about his handsome face.

Still wrapped in a bubble of emotion, Alexandra slowly began to change clothes. Her legs were frozen and she'd worn wet clothes for too long in the snow. Her legs looked mottled and pink as she tried to warm herself by jogging in place. She thought she could see her breath in the air inside her bedroom. The blue skies only meant clearer weather, and without a warming cloud cover, the freeze would set in harder. Already the temperature was dropping.

She wrapped her comforter around herself and walked into the living room. Scott was already in front of the fireplace.

"Think we can recover?" he asked as she sat down beside him.

"We're grownups, right?" She smiled. "I mean, we both know it's career suicide getting involved with someone on the job."

"Right. And we just got caught up in the moment. It's a very romantic place, after all."

Alexandra let out a breath of relief and they fell silent for several moments. "Are you going to sleep out here tonight?" she asked.

"The bedrooms are freezing. I think we ought to set up camp out here where it's warm, don't you?"

"Makes sense. Look, Scott. I worked hard to get where I am. And I haven't had very good luck in the trust department with men."

"I know what you mean about relationships and trust. Boy do I ever." Scott laughed again and the tension between them broke. "Why don't we just try to make the best out of the time we have here? We'll pretend it's a paid holiday or something."

They spent a quiet evening reading while there was light enough. Alexandra knew Scott was acutely aware of her. She certainly knew every move *he* made in the small cabin. Just when she thought she'd buried her attraction to the most inaccessible corners of her mind, all it took was a single movement from him to bring it all rushing back.

It was the way the muscles in his shoulders worked when he threw a piece of wood on the fire. It was that intriguing slant at the corners of those amazing blue eyes. It was his body heat, which she swore she could feel even through her blanket. In a normal situation, she would have gone for a long walk, done anything to avoid thinking of him. But this wasn't exactly a normal situation.

He looked up at her from his book. She felt his gaze before she saw it.

"What?"

"When did your parents die?" he asked.

"Kind of personal, isn't that?"

He waited as she put the book down and tapped the cover with a long glossy fingernail for a moment.

"I was in the second grade. I remember them—at least I have that."

"Siblings?"

"No one. I have friends, mostly Mary. But I'm the one she falls back on when the chips are down, not the other way around."

He lifted a brow. "She's not much of a friend if it's that one-sided."

"It's not that," she said softly. "It's just that I've never tried to find out."

•

He'd studied her face when she'd lifted the book back up, looking away only because he knew he was making her uncomfortable.

When night fell, Scott's thoughts shifted. He couldn't help but notice the way Alexandra's silk pajamas clung. Why couldn't she have worn something loose and flannel? Something that didn't ignite his imagination so thoroughly? Even though she'd quickly wrapped herself in her blanket, his mind repeated the vision again and again.

The pale yellow fabric slid away from her neck when she moved, exposing the creamy skin along her collarbone and down to her shoulder. If only her could hold her for just this one night. He hadn't felt this kind of temptation in years. Maybe he'd never felt it like this at all. Wasn't there more to life than just work? So much more for her just waiting ahead, maybe? There were so many more questions he was dying to ask, but somewhere between them was that invisible boundary line.

"I'll bet you're not very good at truth or dare," he said.

"You'd win that bet."

"Random questions, then?"

She narrowed her eyes at him. "What do you mean?"

Scott smiled. "Random question. What's your favorite color?"

Her eyes closed. "This is dumb." She stayed silent for a minute. "What's yours?"

"Green. See, it isn't that hard. Random question. Do you have any hobbies?"

More silence.

"I like to bowl," he said. "And travel. And play tiddly winks. Definitely that."

She laughed. Laughter was good, he thought.

"Purple, reading, air hockey and shopping. Good night, Scott."

"Good night."

They rolled up in their separate comforters and stretched out in front of the fireplace, gathering near the flames for heat. The temperature outside continued to drop and ice formed in crystalline flakes on the glass inside the cabin windows.

Scott began, "Alex, I can't pretend I don't feel what I feel here." Maybe it was the magic of the nighttime or the glow of the fireplace, but his words took on a life of their own. He'd meant to pretend. Up until two seconds earlier.

"This may sound silly or naïve to you, but I'll explain," she said. "I was engaged to be married once, and one evening I surprised him."

"He wasn't alone," Scott said. He fell silent for a while, then spoke again. "Someone I once thought I loved betrayed me, too."

"Really? Then maybe you know where I'm coming from. See, I really thought he was the only man I would ever be with. I made such a mistake with him and it hurt me both personally and professionally."

"Alex, all men aren't like that. Some of us actually value commitment and respect the woman we're with."

Alexandra rolled over to face him. "Really? So when was the last time you were with a woman? Dated one for a while, slept with her and then ended it? Or how about a convenient one-night stand?"

Scott also rolled to face her. "Is that what you think of me? That I proposition every woman who registers a pulse?"

Alexandra shrugged. "I don't think that, but they do say where there's smoke ..."

Scott cut in before she said something they'd both regret. "That woman I mentioned, Mackenzie—I was with her for over two years and I would have proposed to her. I wanted to. But, I found out some things in time, and let's just say it didn't work out. It would have been disaster. I haven't been with another woman since."

"Oh." Alexandra looked truly taken aback. If anything, at least he wasn't as predictable as she seemed to think all men were.

"In fact," Scott whispered, "I haven't so much as kissed a woman in months, until out there in the snowbank with you today. Empty flings just aren't my style. I left teenage impulsivity behind a long time ago."

Alexandra giggled and tucked a piece of wayward hair behind her ear. "What? No backstage romp with the pop star?"

Scott groaned. "I'm going to physically injure whoever told you those rumors."

"So you beat up on women?" Alexandra gasped in mock horror. "See, I knew I'd find a fatal flaw."

"It was that Sarah, wasn't it?" He groaned again. "I can't win."

Alexandra's eyelids grew heavy and she yawned. One of her long, shapely legs covered in filmy material slid out from under the blanket.

Scott inched closer to her until a mere foot of space kept them apart. "Can I kiss you again, Alexandra Hunter? Nothing sordid. Just one more kiss?"

Her eyes flew open and he watched her gaze drop from his nose down to his lips. Did she want what he wanted? To feel that powerful current again in spite of all the warnings they'd told themselves?

Her look was all the response he needed. He wrapped his hands in her soft hair and pulled her to him. But, she pressed her hands against his chest.

"Scott," she whispered. "Stop. We have to stop. Really!"

He pushed himself away immediately. "I'm sorry, Alex."

"I'm as much to blame as you." She rolled herself up tightly in the blanket and turned away from Scott's view. "Let's just try to get some sleep. No more kissing. No more personal questions, okay? Those lead to bad places."

So much for friendly colleagues, he thought. What he was feeling put "friendly" to shame.

Chapter Five

In the morning light, Alexandra was thinking clearly again—or so she told herself. It was the atmosphere of the night, the romantic novelty of it all, she mentally repeated. Just lust, loneliness and firelight. Still, from the look of the dark circles under Scott's blue eyes, he hadn't slept much during the night. Neither had she, but thank goodness she had the convenience of makeup to hide it.

She wasn't sure if it was good or bad news that came to them across the radio that morning. Though the weather still held fair, it seemed some small thing had broken inside the snowcat. The driver and his mechanic were working frantically to repair it, but the parts they needed weren't scheduled to arrive at the hotel until later that afternoon at best. Scott and Alexandra would be confined to the cabin for another day.

"What's on the agenda for today, Ms. Hunter?" Scott asked, charming her with that crooked grin of his.

"I think a visit to the finest Italian restaurant followed by a shopping spree in the city," she joked. "Seriously, though. I wish I could just get warm. I guess I got chilled during the night."

Scott studied her. "I let the fire burn too low for a couple hours there after I dozed off. Sorry. I can fix it, though."

"Fix what?"

"No, really. I got suckered into going to a day spa once. There was one part of it I liked."

She stared at him.

"Let's give you a visit to heated opulence. Falconer's Mountain Resort. Has a nice ring to it."

Alexandra's muscles were sore from sleeping on the hard wood floor and she had to admit, she was intrigued by anything warm or opulent-sounding at that moment.

"Doesn't it bother you at all that we're sitting up here in the middle of nowhere burning daylight while the enemy camp is probably winning over the client?" she asked.

"Yes. Which is why I'm trying to distract myself."

"Okay, I'll bite," she said. "What are you talking about?"

"We have an entire day to kill here in this cabin, Alex. Let me do something nice for you."

"Can I trust you? Nothing strange planned, right?"

"Just go to your bedroom and wait. Do you have shorts and a T-shirt or something like that with you?"

She nodded that she did.

"Good. Put that on. I'll call you when I'm ready. Now keep your door closed."

Scott had looked so excited that he'd turned this day of virtual imprisonment into a game. She could almost imagine she was on vacation. She slipped on a tank top and her workout shorts and sat on the edge of her bed trying to stay warm. She shivered.

"I'm ready," he called. "Come on out and go get in the bathtub," he commanded. "Go on." He gestured her away playfully. "Get. I promise it'll be good."

Alexandra thought she must have lost her mind. She couldn't remember having felt less stress in years. All she knew was that if he lived up to his word, this was going to feel wonderful. If it was a joke, she'd get even. She stretched out in the cold, porcelain bathtub as Scott came through the door with a bucket full of something white and fluffy. Was he going to dump snow on her? Alexandra started to sit up when a hot, steaming towel dropped across her legs.

"This does feel wonderful," she gasped in surprise, somewhat expecting a joke to follow even still. "It's heaven."

After Scott had left the room and the towels had cooled, Alexandra stepped from the tub and tied the robe tight around her. She blushed furiously as shame surfaced. Duncan had certainly never triggered such a reaction from her. Unease and discomfort crept in. Scott had tried to take care of her—a normal male response, wasn't it? And yet being taken care of was so foreign to her that her emotions simply weren't processing it.

She had to pull herself together—and fast. She showered and dressed, then came back out to the living room as she heard Scott come back in through the door to answer a call coming through on the radio.

The fire blazed in the fireplace, and she sat in front of it. The shivers had stopped.

"Good news! Got the snowcat part in early and are heading up there in a few minutes. Get ready. You won't have to spend another night up there," the driver assured.

Scott left the radio, but his smiled dropped as he looked at Alexandra. "Alex, I'm ..."

She put her hand up to stop his words from leaving his mouth. "Don't say anything. We got caught up in the firelight and the seclusion, but nothing went too far. We have a presentation to give and a client to win. We have to concentrate on that. Just that."

Scott sighed. "What about after the presentation, Alex?"

Alexandra felt another blush threaten and turned away from him. "I think we'd better get ready to go," she whispered. "Reality is what it is, Scott."

"Maybe reality is what you make it."

"Do you ever run out of patience, or not know what you want?"

He simply smiled in return.

Their bags were packed and sitting by the door in very little time. The plow had made its way up to the cabins, and their ride wouldn't be far behind. Soon they heard the sound of the motor chug up the road, and they ran out to meet the driver.

"You two had quite the adventure," called the driver. "Stranded in the mountains. Caught in an avalanche. Bet no one else in your office has that tale to tell."

Alexandra's former demeanor had returned. "Certainly doesn't help us progress much on our business deal, now does it? I imagine the potential client and our rivals have had a wonderful visit down there in the hotel for the past two days."

The driver helped them inside and slammed the door shut. "Nah. The guys from Rio Safari got snowed in at JFK, if you can believe that. Never even made it here. Those three from that other company ain't had nothin' to do except sit in the lounge, stare at each other and hit the bourbon. Talk about a bust."

Alexandra felt a wave of relief pass through her. So Duncan hadn't had the chance to orchestrate an advantage yet. Maybe things were taking a turn for the better after all.

Scott asked, "Did Mac Stevens leave a message of any kind?"

"Just apologies. Guess they'll be calling you later, I'd imagine."

"Great." Alexandra said, trying not to sound too annoyed. After all the time and expense getting here, David wasn't going to be thrilled with the lack of results. She turned to look at Scott and wondered what he'd do if she ran her hand over the black stubble that flowed over his strong jaw line.

The driver continued, "The bright side is that you all have tickets out of this place tomorrow."

Scott nudged Alexandra with his elbow. "Look at it this way—we'll get to know the Zellez team a little more intimately."

"Goody," Alexandra mumbled. "This just keeps getting better and better."

•

When one of the men from Zellez invited Scott and Alexandra to join them for dinner that evening, how could they politely refuse? The man had seemed so sincere and the hotel was nearly vacant due to the blizzard. As the only guests, there was no way Alexandra could have said no without being rude.

She liked two of the men from Zellez and had an easy time talking with them. If Duncan bowed out, the meal might even have a chance at being pleasant.

Alexandra dressed quickly in jeans and a purple turtleneck sweater and ran out to meet Scott in the hall. He walked at her side all the way to the lounge.

"No matter what this Duncan fellow says, don't worry. I've got your back," he assured. "And I won't even let on that I know about his legal shenanigans."

"That's the least of my dread."

The five of them sat together at a rectangular table that was far too large for their small party. Alexandra was grateful she was seated as far from Duncan as the table would allow. The thought of looking at him made her think of throwing something all over again, and this time she'd bet a lovely salad fork would quite literally make a better impression than boxes of takeout.

One of Duncan's companions, a short man named Roger with dark hair and a ruddy complexion, broke the ice. "I suppose this is consorting with the enemy." He lifted his glass in a toast. "Here's to a clean fight."

Scott refilled his glass and joined in the toast. "So tell me, Roger. How long have you been with Zellez?"

"Oh, going on five years now. The company has been really good to us. Mike here has been there seven years, and Duncan started about three years ago. Is that right, Duncan? Three years, isn't it?"

Duncan bobbed his head in affirmation, brought his glass back to his lips and drained the contents. "Three years ago. I can hardly remember what I was doing before that." He ran the back of his hand crudely across his mouth and plunked the empty glass down on the table.

Not missing the jibe, Alexandra sawed into her steak with renewed determination. "Oh, I'm sure it was something rewarding. You've built quite the career, or so it seems." She smiled the type of perfectly polite, icy smile that made Scott glad he was no longer on the receiving end.

The man Roger had referred to as Mike picked up the

conversation. "It must have been pretty alarming to be caught in an avalanche like that. What exactly happened anyway?"

Scott swallowed a bite and said, "Apparently they were supposed to set off a controlled avalanche before we got there, just as a safety precaution. Guess they got the dates wrong, if you can believe that."

"Sounds like a pretty big mix-up to me. Could you even get out of the cabin?" Mike asked.

Alexandra nodded. "We dug out the next morning."

Duncan's eyes were red-rimmed as he refilled his glass. "What did you do that night, I wonder?" He snickered into his drink.

Roger cleared his throat and his face turned even redder than usual. "I'm sure he means what did you do for food and heat? Was there a fireplace?" He shot his colleague a bewildered look.

Alexandra felt Scott grow tense beside her and calmly placed her foot on top of his for just a moment to signal she was all right.

"Yes, Roger, there was a wonderful fireplace and we were fortunate enough to find food stocked in the cupboards." Still the picture of politeness, she turned back to Duncan. "Duncan, I hope this isn't too personal, but I've been meaning to ask you all night about that little scar on your forehead. Is there a fascinating story behind it?"

So Duncan wanted to play games, did he? He was about to meet his match.

Duncan sat silent, looking sullen for a moment before setting down his glass again. "I hit my head on the edge of a coffee table a few years back."

"Oh my," Alexandra declared in wide-eyed innocence. "Why on earth were you under a coffee table?"

Duncan leaned forward. "I wasn't. I turned to see something flying at my head and ducked to avoid it."

Alexandra's insides leapt with victory as the image of Japanese takeout cartons flying through the air at him came to mind. She bet she'd hit him after all. Good.

"Must have been painful."

"No, it was a good evening for me," he said. "I look at this scar and it reminds me of a time when I got rid of a lot of excess baggage and achieved exactly what I'd planned."

Alexandra's hand clenched her fork until her knuckles turned white. The man was admitting he'd conned her and she couldn't do a thing about it. The others at the table looked back and forth between her and Duncan, not understanding what was happening.

•

An uneasy feeling crept over Scott. This conversation was too personal, too vindictive to just be about stolen company secrets. After what they'd shared in the cabin and the conversation they'd had, she would have told him otherwise, wouldn't she?

Duncan pressed on, "I've been noticing something all night, too. When we last met, I could have sworn you had a lovely diamond ring on your finger. No personal tragedy has befallen you, I trust?"

Alexandra's composure held firm. "You're so kind to inquire. But no, I'm afraid the ring you refer to was nothing, just a cheap imitation of the real thing, much like the man who gave it to me, I'm afraid." She addressed the other men at the table with a winsome smile. "I really dodged a bullet with that one." She laughed and winked at them, causing them to laugh in return. Her energy was contagious when she wielded it that way.

After half a dozen drinks and the laughter of his companions assailing his ego, Duncan's poise wasn't so intact. "You weren't woman enough to wear that ring, Alexandra," he spat. "If it hadn't been for your corporate connections, you wouldn't have been able to amuse me in any way while we were together. Oops, I guess you didn't, even at that." Duncan tossed his napkin onto the table. "I'm through with this dinner and I'm through with you."

Duncan staggered to his feet and Scott jumped to his. He had a good idea of what had passed between them, but where he came from, a man didn't treat a woman that way, especially not in public.

"You're not even close to finished," he said. "You owe the lady an apology and I want to hear it now."

Duncan looked Scott up and down, judging his strength and knowing when he was beaten. "My obviously oh-so-sincere apologies," he snarled and tottered out of the room. He knocked against his empty cup as he moved away, and it crashed to the floor without him bothering to pick it up.

Mike and Roger both stood, stammering and red-faced. "We're so sorry. We apologize," they said together several times. "We don't know what could have come over him. Again, let us apologize."

They each spoke a stream of embarrassed sentences in unison, stopping and stumbling over each other's words before running down the hall to catch Duncan.

Scott and Alexandra sat alone at the table. He turned to her, "Duncan was also the man you were involved with, wasn't he?"

Alexandra nodded miserably.

"Why didn't you tell me? We're supposed to be on the same side here. Why didn't you trust me?"

"I don't know, Scott. I didn't really even think to say anything. I just felt so stupid. I mean, take a good look at the guy. Stupid, ugly, stupid beard."

"Tell me what you really think." Scott shook his head. "After all that time in the cabin, you didn't think to tie the pieces together for me? You told me about the stolen documents and then about the man who had hurt you—your former fiancé nonetheless. But, you never had any intention of really letting me know you, did you?"

"Not then. It seemed too personal at the time."

The thought of Duncan, that puffed-up philanderer so much as laying a finger on her beautiful skin, touching and kissing her—the image cut straight through him. How could she have settled for, given herself to a man so undeserving? How could a man like that have betrayed someone so wonderful as Alexandra

Hunter? The world was an upside-down place.

"I'm not sure if you're angry with me or jealous," she said in disbelief. "One thing is for sure, though. We let things go too far in the cabin. We've let personal feelings leak over into business."

"I hope you don't consider that a problem. I don't. I just realized I jumped to a few too many conclusions, Alex. What I know for sure is that you and I have feelings of some sort for each other. Don't you think we should find out where they lead? Come on, forget about Duncan and get to know me better. Heck, for all you know, I really could have been fooling around with celebrities in Europe all my life."

"You don't really think I still believe that, do you?" She ran her hand across her forehead. "Never mind. It doesn't matter. I think Duncan's little display at dinner tonight is an excellent example of exactly why I'm better cut out for a career than a relationship."

"I'm just saying I obviously don't know you well enough yet to have earned your trust, but I can't figure out why you didn't just tell me about Duncan right from the moment we met him here at the hotel. I'm not some dumb cowboy who deserves to be treated with deception."

Even before he finished his last sentence, he wondered if his words were meant for Alexandra, or if they were something he should have said to Mackenzie a long time ago. Scott cringed inside. This was not the untrustworthy Mackenzie he was talking to.

"I'm private that way," she said. "That much you should know by now. And I imagine you understand it."

He saw her recognition of the look his eyes as he recalled a memory of hurt and betrayal. She'd probably seen that same look staring back at her from her mirror.

"I'm sorry, Alex."

"We're both really tired, Scott. I didn't mean to keep anything from you. I just think we've been through a lot the past few days. If I'd been more professional around you in the cabin, you wouldn't feel so strongly about what happened at dinner tonight. See, this is exactly one of the reasons office romances never work. Hey, what happened to 'I've got your back, Alex,' huh? Let's just stick to that."

She smiled soothingly at him, but he paid her little attention.

Scott turned and started to leave the room. "I've still got your back, Alex. I could have pounded Phelps into the ground for a second there. We may not know each other well enough yet, but I already can't stand the thought of him hurting you."

His voice was softer than he would have liked, and yet he didn't turn back to look at her again before he walked away. He didn't know which was worse, the thought of her relationship with Duncan, or the fear that she might not give him the chance to build a relationship of his own with her.

Scott left early the next morning on a flight bound for his home office in Chicago. He needed a couple days to sort things out in his head, and handling some tasks at work seemed a good excuse.

Two years in a relationship with Mackenzie had eroded his trust in love more than he'd imagined. There were no similarities at all between the two women, though. His judgment was clear enough to see that, his pain long enough gone. Mackenzie had stopped at nothing to promote her own financial interests, even playing with his heart and threatening his family in Montana. How would he ever get closer to Alexandra? He was afraid his reaction to Duncan had simply pointed out all of the complications of an office romance to her, and she was finished with him before they'd even started.

•

Alexandra was relieved she'd be taking her return flight to Seattle alone. Just when she started to feel something for him, he'd stepped all over that budding emotion by showing her exactly why personal attachments had no place in the office. Things could get too intense, too fast.

She cursed herself for her unprofessional behavior in the mountain cabin. The heated towels—whatever had possessed her to go along with something so stupid? She'd told herself all along to listen to her head and never her heart, and here was proof of why. No, there was no way she was going to look at Scott Falconer with anything other than professional interest again. The risk was far too great.

"Who am I kidding?" she whispered aloud to herself. "I'm still absolutely crazy about the big jerk." She closed her eyes tightly and shook her head. "I might be in trouble here."

When Alexandra walked into the building, Sarah followed her down the hall to her office like a lost puppy. "Well, well?" She almost jumped up and down with excitement. "You have to tell me the details. What happened in Colorado? Are they from Scott Falconer?"

"Nothing productive happened. And are what from him?" Alexandra was still somewhat irritated with her assistant for all the false rumors she'd planted in her head. She hadn't given Scott a fair initial reaction because of them.

"Those!" Sarah gave a sweeping game show hostess gesture toward Alexandra's office. A dozen long-stem Lady Diana roses sat in a crystal vase in the middle of her desk. She felt the color rise in her face and remembered the emotion in Scott's eyes … She knew without looking that the roses were from him.

"What's the card say?" Sarah squealed, shaking Alexandra back to the present.

Alexandra pulled the card from the bouquet and read it silently to herself. *I've still got your back. I'm sorry.* Thank goodness the card wasn't signed, because she wasn't entirely sure Sarah hadn't done a little snooping.

"Well?"

"They're just from a friendly business associate, that's all," Alexandra told her. "Nothing to get worked up about." She had no intention of reading the card out loud to her assistant no matter how anxious the woman was to hear what was written on it.

Sarah gave her a suspicious and disappointed look and went back to her desk.

Scott called Alexandra just as she sat down at her desk. "Hi, it's me," he said.

"I got the roses. How very original." She hated to shoot him down, but there was no other way.

"Look, Alex. I think I scared you. But I feel wonderful and can't wait to see you. I've asked about Duncan and about your family, but I haven't told you anything you need to know about me. Talk when I get back?"

"No need. We've got to get the presentation going, you know. I don't need to know your past, Scott. What happened in that cabin will never be repeated. It doesn't matter now. I apologize for being to unprofessional with you in Colorado. I wa—"

"You're wrong, Alex," he interrupted. "It matters very much and you know it. We have feelings for each other that are hard to come by in this world. We need to see where they lead."

Alexandra hung up the phone not wanting to hear the end of his romantic sales pitch. He was right. She didn't really know much about him considering all she'd heard. Maybe he was the playboy Sarah had warned her about and happened to be a very good actor when it came to hiding his true self.

That ice wall was firmly in place and she wasn't going to let him chip away at it again. But the man called incessantly, nearly every hour, every day until she wanted to scream. She finally explained to the receptionist that they were working on a presentation together and to expect several calls, but knew that the fodder for office gossip was already in place.

"You have to quit calling," she whispered frantically to him after the fifth call. "Between that and the roses, we may as well have actually done *things* together for all the damage this is doing to my reputation."

"Things?"

"*Things.*"

"Oh, okay. So I won't call you," he agreed amicably.

Five minutes later, Scott appeared in front of her desk. "Surprise! I flew in and came straight here. Go to dinner with me?"

Alexandra's mouth dropped open. "Were you calling from

the parking lot? The plane?" Scott Falconer had nerve if nothing else.

Though she hated to admit it, she hadn't seen him for a couple days, and hadn't realized how much she'd missed looking at his face. He wore a beautifully tailored suit that screamed authority and sophistication. She loved how he could look one way at the office and quite another while tossing wood on a fire. It was as if he stepped with ease back and forth between two very separate, very masculine worlds.

•

Scott grinned. "You're a sight for sore eyes."

Her classic navy blue suit had small yellow buttons and yellow piping at the bottoms of the sleeves—and it fit her amazingly. But no suit could erase the memory of her skin, warmed to golden hues by firelight.

"I missed you," he whispered.

"Shut the door before Sarah hears you," Alexandra hissed. "I'm not having dinner with you. I've put the brakes on where you're concerned, Scott Falconer. Not that they were ever off. Okay, maybe they were off a little." She took a breath to collect herself. "If you'd like to stay here and work on the presentation with me, we can order in pizza or something."

"Alex, I said I'm sorry and I meant it. I'm not typically that intense and I don't want to talk about Colorado any more. But I also don't want to think I damaged what had started between us. You felt it back on the side of the road that first day. I know you did—even then."

"I know you're sincere. And it's fine, really. But business is business and we agreed to keep it that way. From here on out, that is."

Scott sighed. "Dinner? A long conversation? How about a drive down the freeway until we get another flat?"

Alexandra put up her hand and fought to hide a smile. "I don't want to hear any more propositions. Not now. Maybe after the presentation."

"Really? I'll have to add a couple things to my list then." He crossed his arms over his broad chest and smiled.

"I just mean we can talk after the presentation, if you still have the burning need to."

"Oh, I imagine I still will."

•

They worked on the presentation endlessly, sitting side-by-side in front of Alexandra's enormous computer monitor. Scott rolled his chair away when Alexandra signaled he was getting too close, and time after time they jumped when their hands accidentally touched. Reaching across the desk for the stapler or a paperclip took on a level of tension that wouldn't have existed between two other people in the same situation.

"Alex ..." he would start to say in that softened tone she now recognized so well.

"Back to the numbers," Alexandra would instruct without looking up from her desk.

Once while she was typing, Scott looked at her with such an expression of amazement and desire that she almost lost her resolve. His entire being seemed to jump into his blue eyes when he looked at her like that. Pretending not to notice, Alexandra excused herself and walked to the restroom where she locked herself in one of the stalls and stayed there until her hands stopped shaking.

She found tiny gifts hidden in random places throughout her office. A truffle wrapped in red foil was tucked into her tape dispenser. She found a tiny African violet in a new pot beside the other plants on her window. A set of four floating candles shaped like tires miraculously appeared in her filing cabinet. Where in the world he'd found those, she could only guess. Of course, Scott denied any knowledge of the continuously appearing surprises.

He was *courting* her, she realized. Did men even do that anymore?

On a Friday when everyone else had left the office, Scott turned to Alexandra and said, "Come to dinner with me, Alex. I'm hungry. I mean no harm. And I'm sick to death of pizza."

Alexandra studied him for a moment. "Let me get this straight. We're alone in a dark office building, locked away in my office, and you want to leave? Go to a crowded, public restaurant and talk business? I guess that's an indication of your good intentions." She reached for her purse.

"You're flirting with me, Alex." Scott reached out and covered her hand with hers. "Does this mean you're going to let me in again?"

"Do I have a choice?" Her fingers burned where his hand rested on them. "We have to work together." She had nearly forgotten her intent to remain detached from him—so easily forgotten that it scared her.

"Let's date, Alexandra. Let's become involved." He grabbed her roughly by the waist and pulled her against him.

"Are you crazy?" She felt her cheeks sting as her face threatened to redden. She was infuriated that this man had made her blush more times in the past week than she had in her entire life. "You can't keep bringing up this subject while we're working." She struggled to pull away from his hold. "No. No. No."

He nodded and turned her loose. "I've given this more thought than you can imagine. The worst that can happen is I'll go back to Chicago, you'll stay here and it will just end. We'll be discrete and if it doesn't work out, we'll survive. Reputations intact," he assured.

"It's not just avoiding an office romance, Scott. After all that happened, I don't trust myself with you." She wasn't used to such emotional honesty. She looked down at her desk.

"Then trust *me*. I'm looking for the commitment, Alex. I won't let things go so far that you'd regret it the next morning."

"But what about you?" she countered. "If we become involved, won't you always wonder if I did it to keep you pliable so that I get my way on the presentation?"

"It's a chance I'll take."

"I can't, Scott."

He shrugged in temporary resignation. "Well, then it's back

to friendly colleagues for now."

"Well, yes and no. I think we could safely go out together just once." Alexandra put her purse down and opened up her desk drawer. She pulled out an envelope with the words *You're Invited* printed in swirling gold foil.

"I got this in the mail today," she said. "It's from Mac Stevens. Four tickets to Rio's annual holiday gala with the request of our illustrious presence."

"Pick you up at seven?" he asked.

Chapter Six

Mary was ecstatic. "You're giving it a shot? I can't believe it! Ms. Social Recluse on a date." She handed Alexandra a cup of coffee and sat down next to her at the kitchen table.

"He's picking me up any minute now. It's not a date, not a real one anyway. It's for work, and David and his wife are going with us."

Mary waved her hand back and forth. "A double date then. It's romantic. Forbidden office romance."

"It's not a romance. We stopped that before it got out of hand."

The other woman rolled her eyes and slapped her hand against her forehead. "You mean you stopped it. For the last time—he's not Duncan, so why put the brakes on? From the sounds of things, he's just an amazing guy who can somehow rattle you out of that controlled shell. Count your blessings that you've found someone who can jostle your molecules. You need that. Heck, we *all* need that."

"Mary!" Alexandra grimaced and then ran to the window at the sound of a car pulling into the driveway. "He's here. Be good."

Mary stuffed a bagel in her mouth, tossed Alexandra a breath mint, and slipped her jacket on as Scott came through the door. "No hanky panky, now," she called as she walked around him and made her exit.

Alexandra shook her head. "That was Mary."

Scott laughed. "So I gathered." He leaned in and kissed her on the cheek. "You look ..."

"So do you," she whispered.

"Well, Date, do you think our work will suffer because of this sordid holiday affair?"

"Are you kidding?" She grinned. Her work suffer? Ever since he'd come back to town after their trip to Colorado, she couldn't wait to get to the office. She was at her desk even earlier than usual and stayed later than she needed, all in hopes of just an extra five minutes she could justify with Scott. And with all her newfound nervous energy, she juggled everything at once and found more to do.

Scott made her feel alive at work. Being near him was like the rush she got from closing a new deal, and he was going to be very hard to resist in that tuxedo. He looked so strikingly masculine and so supremely confident in it that Alexandra had to look away before he caught her admiring him openly.

Alexandra held tightly to her little satin clutch. David and his wife rode in the front, chatting away, and leaving the backseat to him and Alexandra. The heat as they drove along was suddenly electric and stifling. She felt their energy move back and forth between them in waves, and was so ready to jump from the car that she almost didn't wait until Scott opened the door for her. When she stepped from the car, she looked down and noticed Scott's shiny black cowboy boots on the pavement. That he'd chosen to wear them even with a tuxedo made her smile, and knowing that she approved made him smile back.

She slid her slender arm around his hard, muscular one, allowing herself to be escorted to the door. Rio Safari had literally rolled out a red carpet for their guests.

"I feel like a movie star arriving at a premiere," Alexandra said.

Crystal chandeliers and champagne flutes sparkled around the room. A band on the other side of the ballroom played a waltz and couples dressed elegantly all swayed in a mix of colors around the floor. A full bar and several exquisitely decorated tables full of hors d'oeuvres and ice sculptures lined an entire wall.

"Should we split up and mingle?" Alexandra asked. "Or should we stick together for a while?" She turned to Scott, who nodded to show her that David had already almost disappeared in the crowd.

•

Scott was simply awestruck. Her hair, full of shining reds and browns, was piled loosely high up on her head with elegant little tendrils escaping down around her neck. She'd used smoky eye shadow and burgundy lipstick for the evening, and they transformed her normally striking features into something sensual.

And that dress—he couldn't take his eyes off the way the dark copper velvet flowed down her body or the way a graceful slit in the fabric opened to expose one leg.

He breathed in the familiar, lush scent of her perfume oil. "I'm for staying together as long as possible." The soft lighting glowed across the creamy skin of her throat and he had to force away the desire to bend down and softly kiss her neck.

As he gazed at Alexandra, something caught his attention from across the room and he sighed reluctantly. "Get ready," he warned. "Brace yourself. This isn't going to be pretty."

That little vertical stress line appeared on Alexandra's forehead and didn't fade when she saw the object of Scott's attention.

Weaving through the crowd toward them, a woman waved her arm high and shouted, "Scott, darling. Is that you?"

The woman's hair was such a pale shade of blond that it was almost white. It was pulled starkly back from her face, a style that served to accentuate her catlike eyes, tiny nose and full red lips. Her royal blue gown plunged deeply in the front, showcasing a stunning diamond necklace and ample curves.

She embraced Scott with enthusiasm, pulled him away from Alexandra, and kissed him on both cheeks.

He pulled back quickly from the woman's embrace and with

his arm reaching around Alexandra's back, just as quickly pulled her back to his side.

"Alexandra, I'd like you to meet Mackenzie Stevens, CEO of Rio Safari."

Mac Stevens looked Alexandra up and down and her icy blue eyes narrowed.

"Alexandra Hunter," she said, "it's certainly interesting to see you in person." She hadn't missed the turning heads of every male in the room when Alexandra walked through the door. In fact, she had only noticed Scott standing there when she'd turned to see what the stir was about.

Mac gave a cold little laugh and turned her back to Alexandra. "Scott, darling. I'll talk with you later. I simply must go greet someone important right now."

Alexandra took Scott's arm again, more tightly than necessary. "Your Mackenzie is Mac Stevens? The woman you almost proposed to? *Her*?"

Scott noticed the confusion in Alexandra's eyes. "I tried to tell you Alex, remember?" he said gently. "I know how you must feel. I felt the same way when I found out exactly who Duncan had been to you. Remember?"

Alexandra felt a ridiculous show of disappointment and jealousy threaten to find its way to her expression. She silently chastised herself. Hers was certainly a silly, emotional reaction for someone allegedly unwilling to explore any romantic feelings for Scott. For two years that frozen, blond viper had been part of Scott's life, and from the looks of things, she'd like to be again. She cringed at the thought of Scott touching another woman.

"Random question. What's going through your head right now?"

"I'm *fine*," she lied obviously. "But I think we should mingle now." She moved just out of Scott's reach, his fingers sliding from around her waist as she walked away. She gave him a tight little smile.

"You're *jealous*!" He laughed in shock.

Scott watched as Alexandra made her way through the

crowd, stopping to greet Mike from Zellez and then talking with another couple he didn't recognize. The light from the chandeliers flickered against the warm tones of her hair and set off the soft cream color of her skin. She was amazing to watch in action. Scott couldn't have mingled if he tried. He was completely captivated and wasn't sure if his legs could even move.

Scott watched as Alexandra sank farther into the crowd and then finally followed her while he still had the chance. She wasn't going to dismiss him that easily even though he suspected, all business excused aside, she was just protecting herself from another broken heart. He'd never seen someone so guarded. Then he looked up and saw Duncan, pompous thing that he was, slowly approaching her like a poisonous animal stalking its prey. He was just waiting to spoil her evening one way or another, waiting to assault her before she even noticed he was there.

•

Alexandra had draped herself in her most poised and self-assured façade. She knew no other way to get through the evening without thinking of the jealousy that just blindsided her. She knew Scott had tried to tell her about his relationship with Mac Stevens and she'd brushed his explanations aside thinking it couldn't matter. And now suddenly it did matter.

The Alexandra of a month ago would have called it an advantage to have the potential client enamored of someone on her team. But now Alexandra found it irritating. So this was the connection he had with the CEO of Rio Safari. What was the plan anyway? To seduce a contract out of Mac Stevens?

As Alexandra stepped by him in her bedazzled satin heels, Scott caught up to her, reached out and grabbed her by the arm, pulling her back to him.

"What do you think you're doing?" she whispered in disbelief. She smiled brightly while looking around to see who around them had noticed.

"I'm taking you out to the dance floor." He smiled a little too brightly at her as they moved with the music. "Thought we'd give this dancing thing a whirl."

"You know, dancing with your presentation partner isn't part of the job description," she said.

"I'd call it more of a fringe benefit."

The orchestra played slowly and their bodies swayed together in a sensual rhythm. This was torment, she thought, and started to question the wisdom of ever showing him that invitation in the first place.

She tried her best to steel herself against the warm, flowing sensations Scott's body near hers created. The soft glow from the chandeliers overhead did nothing to lessen the effect of his gaze. Why couldn't he be some tall, dark stranger she had met just this night? She could run away with him and do things only other women dared to do. Things she never dared to do herself.

"Penny for your thoughts," Scott whispered into her ear.

Alexandra lifted an eyebrow. "You think my thoughts come that cheap?"

He held her hand tightly and spun her around with flair. "I think you're priceless."

Alexandra looked away from his face. The top of her head level was with his broad chest, but the view there wasn't any safer. "It's not going to do any good for business if we only spend time together tonight. We can cover twice as much ground if we split up, you know."

When the music finally ended, they stopped dancing and simply stood together on the dance floor surrounded by other couples. The attraction between them was almost tangible. Alexandra's heart pounded wildly. She had to get far, far from him before she gave herself and her feelings away and threw her arms around him right in the middle of the dance floor.

"Time to mingle," she said suddenly and stepped back from his embrace.

Alexandra lost track of Scott in the room. There were simply too many guests dancing and talking, and she was trying her best not to look for him. She found herself enjoying the evening with half her thoughts lost somewhere with Scott as it was. As she looked from face to face in conversation, part of her imagined the structure of his cheekbones, his inky black eyelashes, the way the corners of his lips curved up. Alexandra was glad for the distraction such a large social gathering had to offer. She barely had time to pop a stuffed mushroom and a shrimp puff into her mouth before someone else asked her to dance. She was glad though—she thought she'd caught a glimpse of Duncan hovering near the hors d'oeuvres and didn't want to waste a single breath of air talking to him.

She had to give Mac Stevens credit for one thing, though. The woman definitely knew how to put a brilliant guest list together. Inside of an hour, Alexandra had managed to collect the business cards of half the elected officials in the state, not to mention an entire stack of cards from people belonging to one board of directors or another. The night was still young when she managed to grab a glass of water and another shrimp puff, and slip out into the courtyard for a few minutes of fresh air.

•

Scott looked around the room and couldn't see Alexandra anywhere. He realized they needed to mingle, but he swore she'd spent the evening intentionally avoiding him. He saw her whirling around the ballroom floor first with one partner and then the next. Whenever she would swirl close enough for him to touch, she would just as quickly spin away in a blur of copper light. He had last seen her with a senator who had a reputation worse than his own, except he knew for a fact that the senator had actually earned his.

He didn't miss the attention Alexandra drew wherever she moved. Men turned their eyes toward her with unveiled appreciation, though she never seemed to take notice. Older women in the room admired her beauty with smiles and the younger ones shot looks of envy in her direction. It was amusing almost, but it also reinforced his opinion of what a remarkable woman Alexandra Hunter was.

Scott hadn't missed Mac eyeing him from across the room,

either. He hated the way she'd greeted him as if nothing wrong had ever passed between them. He hated the way she'd been so blatantly rude to Alexandra. How could he not have seen the money-hungry, shallow woman Mackenzie was bent on becoming, even while they were together? Her character was so obvious to him now. He was pulled from his thoughts by a long, red fingernail running down his biceps.

"Scott, darling. You have no idea how I've longed to see you again." She was the picture of icy beauty with no warmth beneath the surface. Fake. Fake. Fake.

Scott moved away from her touch. How she could feign such friendliness after the last time they'd spoken was beyond him. "I'm only interested in business, Mackenzie. Just business."

Mac Stevens looked up with a hurt expression that Scott knew from experience she didn't really feel. "I'll bet you might have other ideas if you hadn't arrived with such a distraction on your arm."

"You really don't change, do you? Alexandra Hunter and I are business partners working on a presentation for you. It was not my decision."

Mac smiled coolly. "Oh, I know that. Ms. Hunter's proposal was excellent. But all that aside, when I heard you'd joined D. W. Songstram, too, it was icing on the cake."

"I don't like being played with, Mackenzie."

"Why did you leave me over such trifling matters, Scott? We were such a good team."

Scott laughed outright. "Trifling? Good? What a joke. You tried to steal the land my father worked his entire life to make something of. I think that alone should be reason enough."

She put her hand on his arm again. "I miss you, Scott. We really were so good together. Think about it. Think how much time we could spend together if your company gets the contract."

"We were finished a long time ago, Mackenzie. I don't care to repeat past mistakes. I was hoping since we know each other, it could be beneficial professionally. That's all." How naive had he been? Good together? He barely remembered any of the feelings he'd once felt for her, much less her touch. The mere thought seemed very unappealing now. He thought that curling up with one of those ice sculptures would be warmer.

Mac laughed and touched her flawless forehead to Scott's arm, all melodrama and image. "Silly, darling. Don't say things you don't mean." She squeezed his biceps and gave a suggestive little noise. "You always have been such a man, haven't you? So rugged ..."

•

Alexandra set her water glass down on a bench just before she noticed Scott standing inside in a darkened corner with Mac Stevens. She looked up in time to see the woman run her hand suggestively down his arm. What was it that Scott has professed in the cabin about understanding betrayal and looking for commitment? Now he stood there having a drink and laughing with his former girlfriend. Mac Stevens had her hands all over him, and he just stood there when he could have walked away at any given moment. Finally the blond wiggled away and Alexandra could see that her blue gown was not only frontless, but backless—cut all the way down to indecency on a body that was obviously well cared for. It was probably the only thing Mac truly loved, now that Alexandra thought of it.

She sighed deeply and sunk down on the bench. Romance and business never mixed, she repeated for the hundredth time.

David stepped out into the courtyard. "Alex, I've been looking all over for you."

She put on her best smile. "I just needed a little air." Even in the mild winter air, she felt a little warm, maybe even a little flushed.

"You danced up quite a storm in there," he said. "Meet anyone interesting?"

She patted her little handbag stuffed with business cards. "A whole stack. Sending out the 'it was nice to meet you' notes should be enough to keep Sarah away from the water cooler all week." She gave David a soft smile.

David looked at her more closely. "I've never seen my vice

president without a glint in her eyes before tonight. Is something wrong, Alex?"

"Honestly, I'm feeling a little sick to my stomach right now."

Scott appeared from out of the ballroom and stopped beside David. Alexandra looked away.

David patted the younger man on the shoulder and said, "Connie and I are going to drinks with the senator. Oh, the tales I imagine he could tell. Should be an interesting evening. Here, take my car and drive Alexandra home if she's ready." He tossed the keys to Scott and walked away with his arms wrapped around his wife.

Scott and Alexandra were silent on the way home. "You aren't speaking to me?" Scott asked. "What happened?"

"I'm sorry. Was there something you wished to discuss?" That rolling feeling in her stomach wasn't going away. Maybe she'd finally succeeded in giving herself an ulcer.

Scott pulled the car over to the side of the road and turned to her. "Look, Alex. I'm sorry. I really wanted to tell you about Mackenzie. I tried to, in fact."

"Your personal life is none of my business, Scott." Her back was rigid against the seat. "That's not it at all."

"I don't have any feelings for Mackenzie Stevens. Not any positive ones, anyway. I promise I've never lied to you." He lifted back that strand of hair that always seemed to fall across her face.

"I can't talk to you about this now," Alexandra whispered, placing one hand over her stomach.

"Alex—"

"No, really. I can't." Alexandra fumbled with the handle, swinging the door open just before she leaned over in her seat and became extraordinarily ill onto the pavement outside.

Chapter Seven

Scott knew a case of food poisoning when he saw one. After a trip to the emergency room, the wee hours of the morning had already come around before Scott pulled David's car safely into Alexandra's garage.

Stomach still on edge, Alexandra leaned heavily on Scott as he walked her inside, stopping now and again to catch her breath and curse the existence of all shrimp puffs in general. She couldn't remember having ever felt so sick in her life. Why did it have to be in front of this gorgeous man?

Her insides convulsed and rebelled, and a fever caused by the bacteria made her feel light-headed. Her entire body ached for that matter. The doctors had given her an I.V. at the hospital because every time she tried to take a sip of water, her stomach rejected it. If she'd felt any better, vanity would have kicked in. But right now, she needed Scott there with her no matter how bad she looked.

He helped her unzip her dress, and though tempted to peek, he turned politely away while she slipped into a purple nightshirt with script across the front. *Cats. Books. What else is there?*

He shook his head. She didn't have any pets, did she? And he'd also have to ask his father to remind him of exactly what the benefits of being a gentleman were when watching a woman as stunning as Alexandra undress was at stake.

Scott stretched out on the bed beside her and smoothed

back her hair. He ran a cool washcloth along her hot forehead as she drifted off into sleep. Not sure if she even knew he was still there, he kissed her sweetly on top of her head.

Alexandra smiled. "If you wanted to get me into bed, there had to be an easier way than this," she murmured.

Scott laughed and watched over her while she slept. Her thick hair had come out of its style and cascaded softly around her shoulders. Her makeup had long since been wiped away and her face was flushed with fever. Yet even with all that and her obvious lack of minty fresh breath, Alexandra was still the most dazzling woman Scott had ever seen. He couldn't stop looking at her as she slept. Never once had he felt that way with Mackenzie. In fact, looking back he realized that though he had initially been struck by her cool brand of beauty, the good times he spent with her had been shades of gray compared to even the simplest conversation with Alexandra.

The contrast was remarkable. Mackenzie feigned warmth, but in reality was the equivalent of a human iceberg. Alexandra feigned reserve to mask the warm, sensitive woman she truly was.

He brushed his lips against her forehead and said what he couldn't say when she was awake. "What did I do to deserve you?" he whispered. "I think I'm falling for you, Alexandra Hunter."

•

Mary let herself in the next morning and found Scott, still in his tuxedo shirt and pants, asleep on top of the covers beside Alexandra. Her fingers wrapped securely around his hand as she slept.

Mary tapped Scott on the shoulder and whispered, "I got your message." She tilted her head toward the bathroom and tossed him a T-shirt and pair of sweat pants. "Sorry, those were all I could dig up. Go take a shower and get cleaned up. You don't smell so good."

Scott crawled stiffly off of the bed and stumbled into the bathroom. Mary shook her head in amazement. There was no way a man would stay with a woman through a night like that if he didn't have some very real feelings for her. And from the look of Alexandra, she hadn't exactly been a prize catch these past few hours.

Alexandra rolled over in the bed and squinted at Mary standing there. "Scott, you look worse than I do in the morning."

"Very funny," Mary hissed. "Do you know that man stayed with you the entire night?"

Alexandra nodded, still feeling like she was getting over a case of the flu. "I remember." The recollection of her gastrointestinal pyrotechnics flashed through her mind and she rolled over and moaned. "What a horrible party."

Scott emerged from the shower wearing a pair of sweats that were far too short. "It's alive," he announced and then shot Alexandra another tentative look. "Sort of." He ducked a flying pillow and continued, "I've got to get David's car back to him. I'll stop by the office and pick up your mail and faxes. How about I bring them by later in the morning? I hope you weren't thinking of trying to come in."

"I think I'll stay put for another day." She dropped her head back against the firm mattress, regretting she'd thrown her best pillow at him.

When Scott had gone, Alexandra stumbled into the bathroom and examined herself in the mirror. She thought of the beautiful, blond Mac Stevens from the evening before.

"Oh, Alexandra," she said to herself, "what a nightmare."

•

Scott stood in front of the fax machine that Monday morning, scarcely believing what he'd just read. He held in his hands a memo from Mac Stevens to all of the shortlist presenters. That woman was a real piece of work, he thought. She'd certainly wasted no time distributing the memo after the party. In fact, it looked as if she'd sent it just after he'd left with Alexandra. He considered crumbling the paper up in his hand and pretending it had never arrived.

The fax announced that the presentation had been

postponed yet another two weeks, but that wasn't the part that troubled him. Alexandra's role had essentially been wiped out with one simple, manipulative, premeditated request. It seemed Rio Safari wanted to hear only one presenter speak from each company—the most senior ranking member of the team. No one else would be allowed in the room. It was to be Scott facing the review panel without Alexandra. If Rio's board of directors had known what Mackenzie was up to, they would have never agreed to something so unprofessional.

He again fought the urge to squash the fax and throw it into the wastebasket. This wasn't a business decision by any stretch. This was one-hundred-percent Mackenzie Stevens eliminating what she perceived as the female competition—as if Mackenzie could even begin to compete with Alexandra.

"Sarah," he called out as he rounded the corner, "could you get Mac Stevens on the line for me?" He tossed her number on Sarah's desk. "I'll take it in Alexandra's office."

"Scott, darling," came the sultry voice on the other end of the phone. "I knew you'd be calling."

"I need to see you, Mackenzie." He shut the door to Alexandra's office. "We need to talk about this fax I just received."

"What's there to talk about? Some of the Board members and I thought it best to keep the presentation as uncluttered as possible. That's the way it is. Unless you're not up to the challenge?"

"You know that's not why I called. I know your old moves, Mackenzie, and this one seems very familiar."

Mac made an unconcerned little noise. "If you're prepared, then I can't imagine what your concern might be, darling. And you know it would be a conflict of interest to meet privately with you at this stage. But, I'll see you before the presentation and hopefully after ..." Her voice held an unwelcome suggestive tone.

Scott slammed down the phone, picked up his jacket, and headed out to do the inevitable—break the news to Alexandra.

•

Alexandra was out of bed and feeling much improved when Scott pulled up in her driveway. She couldn't remember the last time she'd taken a day of sick leave and just relaxed. But, when Scott came to the door with a single fax in his hand instead of a pile of mail, a feeling of foreboding crept over her.

His hair was rumpled from where he'd run his hand through it too many times and his expression was far too serious. He tossed his jacket and the fax onto her sofa and pulled Alexandra into his arms, burying his face in her hair.

"I should never have joined this project. I never should have said yes. I should have known she wasn't capable of professionalism. What you were afraid of has happened, and I—"

"Scott ..." she started to say as his mouth came down over hers. Her knees weakened as he kissed her until her strength dissolved.

"Alexandra, do you know what you do to me?"

She wrapped her arms around his neck and kissed him back, her body moving of its own accord tighter against him. "I couldn't stand seeing her touch you like that," she whispered. As soon as the words were spoken, a tiny voice in the back of her mind wondered why she'd confessed that. She pulled slightly away and fought to catch her breath.

"I would *never* hurt you, Alex. Never."

She leaned in to kiss him again and he moved away reluctantly, remembering the reason he had come before she pushed him past the point of being able to think at all. He traced her lips with his finger. "I hate this. I really do, but you need to take a look at this fax."

Still shaking from his touch, Alexandra drew another deep breath and picked up the fax. Slowly she scanned the words on the paper, scarcely believing what she read with her own eyes. There in black and white, her greatest fear from the beginning had taken shape. She'd let down her guard, and somehow, somewhere along the way, this man had infiltrated her project and taken away something she'd put half a year of her life into.

She sank down onto the sofa. "Get out of here," she said calmly. "I need to be alone for a while."

It all made sense to her now. She remembered Scott and Mac Stevens together at the party. The too-familiar touches, the secret discussion in the corner, their laughter—all of it fit together. Had they intended from the very beginning what she now suspected? Scott knew that securing a multi-million-dollar contract with Rio would be a feather in the cap of any executive. But to steal her project away from her, all the while professing feelings of love? It was unimaginably cruel, this scheme he and Mac must have planned.

Scott looked at her in confusion. "I knew you'd be angry, which is why I wanted to tell you as soon as I could. We'll figure out a way to either get around this or fix it. Somehow."

His words rang hollow inside her cloud of hurt. "Well, I hope you and the presentation will be very happy together," she said.

"Alexandra, surely you don't think I had anything to do with this?"

"I saw you two. This was planned all along, wasn't it? Congratulations." She sighed as she opened the door behind him.

"Alex, this is all Mackenzie. I had no idea she'd try something like this."

"I asked you to leave."

She shut the door behind him and locked it for good measure. Mackenzie Stevens could have him. The two of them were obviously a match made in Hades anyway.

•

Alexandra settled into one of the posh leather chairs in David's office as he leaned on the corner of his desk. She'd thought about her request all morning long and waited until the end of the day to talk to David about it.

"You want a new assignment?" he asked in surprise.

"Yes. Considering the way the Rio project has shaken out, it seems my involvement is to be rather limited. I've given Falconer all the information I can and short of actually presenting, there's not much more I can do."

David studied her for a moment. So she was back to calling him Falconer, was she? "I was as surprised as you were when Mac Stevens sent that fax limiting our team to one presenter, so I can understand your request."

"I'd like to find something to put my energies into. Anything hot right now?"

David walked around behind his desk and sat down. "If you'd asked me yesterday, that's exactly what I'd have talked to you about. But this morning I happened to get a call from one of the men on Rio's board of directors. I wouldn't say anything to anyone outside this office about how I know this, but it looks like you're not off the hook just yet."

"What do you mean?"

"Well," David said, "I got the impression that this particular Rio board member was none too pleased with the Stevens fax. There have been a lot of inconsistencies in this process, so they've scheduled a pre-presentation meeting—sort of a last chance for all the competitors to ask questions and get equal treatment."

Equal treatment, she thought. *What a joke.* "So Falconer and I need to go as a team?"

David nodded. "He also indicated they're issuing a follow-up fax today. They don't want to publicly step on Mac Steven's toes by inviting the full team to speak again, so they're instead asking for everyone to be available outside the room in case of questions."

"Just what I've always wanted to do—sit out in the hall and wait for someone else to present my work."

"Try not to take it personally, Alex. Looks like you and Scott are stuck with each other for a few more days. At least we know Rio is keeping a close watch on the whole situation."

Alexandra's heels clicked along the tile floor more slowly than usual on her way back to the office. The sound used to seem filled with a sense of purpose, but now each step only carried her closer to an office cluttered with the corpse of her project.

•

Scott saw Alexandra walking down the hall without that sense of lovely determination she always carried so lightly. He cursed Mackenzie under his breath, and then cursed himself. If he hadn't accepted David's offer, if David hadn't heard through the grapevine that he knew Mac personally, then he could have spared Alexandra the anguish she was going through. He should have said no. How stupid had he been to think Mac might be professional, or that the rest of the Board might keep her in line.

He knew what Alexandra must think of him. Everything he'd promised her would never happen, had happened. Scott also knew what he would have to do. First, he had to find a way to convince Alexandra his professional intentions were honorable, and then he had to find a way to make her fall in love with him. Then he had an idea—a brilliant one he thought.

Alexandra looked as though her thoughts were far away, so it had to come as even more of a shock when he grabbed her by the arm and pulled. The next thing he knew, she was seated awkwardly beside him atop several boxes of paper inside a small supply closet.

Scott snapped the door shut and locked it from the inside. He hoped his idea was as brilliant as it first seemed.

"Are you crazy?" she yelled.

A single stripe of light from under the door made it hard to see him in the dark. "Shh," he cautioned. "What do you think people will do if we make noise and they discover us locked together in a supply closet? Could start some pretty nasty rumors."

Alexandra imagined the faces of her coworkers and rolled her eyes. "Isn't this illegal imprisonment or something?" she whispered.

"Probably. I don't care. You haven't exactly been willing to talk to me since that stupid fax arrived."

"You mean since you stole my project. Or to use your colorful expression, 'horned in' on it."

Scott put his hands on her shoulders. "You have to listen to me, Alex. Really hear me. I had nothing to do with that decision. It's ludicrous, but when Mackenzie saw you walk in that room looking the beautiful, stunning way you did, her claws came out."

Alexandra probably had a hard time imagining Mac Stevens feeling threatened by anyone. "I saw you together in the corner conspiring."

"Conspiring?" Scott almost laughed. "Is that what you think?" The scent of her perfume oil was intoxicating in the small closet.

Alexandra stayed silent until she heard the clunk of footsteps outside pass. "You're going to get us both fired." The closet was extremely small—getting smaller by the minute—and he was too close to her.

Alexandra continued. "Let's look at the facts here. I spent six months on a project only to hear that you're coming in at the last minute and I need to share it. We work together for a while until I get comfortable with you and then I find out your real connection to the client. And then—oh, this gets better. And then I see you all cozy with your former lover and voilà, Alexandra is off the project and out of the picture two days later. Who has the entire project now? Why, none other than Mr. Scott Falconer."

Scott's jaw dropped. "I suppose you think I deliberately poisoned your shrimp puffs, too."

"It's a distinct possibility." Her chin was high again. If anything, he knew how to put the fighting spirit back into her.

He moved closer to her so that her knees brushed against his thighs. She tried to move farther back on the stack of boxes and couldn't. He leaned in and placed his hands on the boxes—one on either side of her.

"Think about this," he whispered. "If my goal was to take the project, why wouldn't I have done it from the beginning?" His lips were so close to hers that he could feel her breath. "If there was a big conspiracy, why wouldn't I have had Mackenzie just send a fax when I was hired and request that I give the presentation right from the start?"

•

Alexandra's anger was treacherously close to melting away from her. How dare he poke holes in her theory this way? He made sense on some level and on another, a sense of shame crept in. She hadn't treated him fairly, but there was no time to think about it. Scott's lips had already found hers.

All she wanted to do was lay back on the boxes and forget everything. She had been so tired, so angry and so untrusting for much too long. Scott had been good to her even when she least deserved it and it felt as if his touched healed her somehow.

"Do you believe me, Alex?" he murmured against her lips.

She nodded that she did.

"I want you to promise me something." He pulled away and looking deeply into her eyes. "The next time you suspect something sinister or start to distrust me, I want you to wait and give me a chance. Okay?"

"All right."

She gently pushed him away and slid off of the boxes, surprised she could stand without wobbling. "We still have the same problem," she whispered into his ear. "We work together."

Her argument sounded thinner every time she used it.

Scott wrapped his arms around her tightly and held her against his chest for what seemed hours. "I look at it this way, Alex. A job like mine is easy to find. A woman like you isn't."

Alexandra felt warmth spread from head to foot as she embraced him. "We got off to a really strange start, didn't we?" She turned her head and looked up at him with eyes that glittered with desire. "After the presentation, we'll see what happens."

As they looked at one another, the last bit of light disappeared as the beam underneath the door went out and the office noises outside faded away. Could the workday have ended so soon?

They stood there in each other's arms afraid to move. "Think everyone has gone?" Scott whispered.

"I don't hear anyone. Hope there aren't any stragglers. Try the door."

Scott unlocked the latch on their side of the door and put his hand on the knob. The door didn't open. He turned it again and the door still refused to budge.

"Uh-oh," he said. "I think it's locked from the outside, too."

"I didn't hear anyone lock it. Let me try." Alexandra pulled in vain on the handle. "Think we could break it?"

"Oh yeah, and who's going to explain the damage tomorrow?"

"We have two choices then. Mary or Sarah," Alexandra said as the lights on her cell phone illuminated the dark closet. She held her finger over the luminous number pad in anticipation.

They looked at each other and said in unison, "Mary."

It took Mary more than an hour to find Alexandra's spare office key at her house, track down a screwdriver, and make her way to the office.

Alexandra and Scott leaned against opposite corners of the supply closet as they listened to Mary remove screw after screw to take the entire doorknob and lock out of the door.

When the door flew open, Mary simply stood there with the screwdriver in her hand surveying the guilty captives inside. "Either of you feel like explaining?" she teased. From the looks of their disheveled clothing and tousled hair, no explanations were really necessary. At least there was no one around the office to witness the scene.

Scott said, "You two go on home. I'll put the door back together and head out in a minute."

"I had to take the bus," Mary announced. "Looks like you get to drive me home, Ms. Alexandra." Her face held a knowing, smug look as she clasped her hands behind her back and smiled.

"Not a word," Alexandra warned as they drove. "I don't want to hear a thing."

Mary shrugged, grinning all the while. "Who? Me? I wasn't going to say anything. On second thought, what's the going rate for a good blackmail payoff these days?"

"Not funny. What am I going to do, Mary? I'm breaking all

my own rules with a guy I barely know."

"Good. Need any pointers?"

•

Mac Stevens was conspicuously absent from the pre-presentation meeting at Rio Safari International the next morning. Of even greater significance, the third team had announced their formal resignation from the presentation, narrowing the competition down to two firms.

Scott and Alexandra arrived side by side with an enhanced charisma together that couldn't be ignored. They had survived flat tires, an avalanche, food poisoning, a wicked misunderstanding and an evening locked together in a supply closet. A formal client meeting was a cakewalk by comparison, even with Duncan in the room looking daggers in their direction.

"I could quit," Scott had offered. "I hadn't thought of it before, but I'm willing."

"No," she'd said. "At this point in the game, the client would dump us if you did." But she'd appreciated the gesture.

They had come to work marvelously together, each tuned in to the same questions and same streams of thought during the discussion. There was no doubt in their minds that the presentation they had prepared was right on the mark.

Earlier that morning, the graphics department had brought over the final poster boards with their enormous illustrations. Alexandra had even hooked up the projector to her laptop to watch the computerized part of the presentation animate its way across the wall of her office. This was quite possibly the best piece of work she had ever done, and though a twinge went through her when she thought of handing it over to Scott, she could picture him in his naturally charming way using her images and his wizardry with numbers to win over the Rio Safari panel.

Her attention returned to the meeting. Alexandra hated to be wrong, but she had to admit to herself that David had known all along exactly what D. W. Songstram Corporation needed to win the client. Mackenzie hadn't been the only factor in Scott's hiring, David had quietly told her.

•

When the members of the review team from Rio left the room, Scott grabbed a donut and a cup of coffee from a refreshment table, while an obviously smitten Roger and Mike from Zellez had found a way to lure Alexandra into conversation.

Duncan sauntered over to Scott with his hands plunged into his pockets. "Looks like it's come down to you against me next week, doesn't it, Falconer?"

"You mean it's down to your team against our team," Scott corrected. He was convinced he'd probably like to strangle the guy even if he hadn't known about his past with Alexandra.

Duncan ran his hand across his goatee. "No, not really. I think we both know who the real leaders are. Mike and Roger are just a means to an end. Gotta have someone to do the grunt work, right? And Alexandra has always been a piece of fluff. It's no wonder Mac didn't care to listen to her drone on and on in a presentation."

Scott clenched his crumbling donut too hard and had to set it back down on the table. "If there wasn't a room full of people here right now, I'd beat the tar out of you."

Duncan took a step back and put both his hands up with his palms facing Scott. "Man, with a temper like that, it's no wonder Mac dumped you. Kicked the garbage to the curb, I guess. She's found a better man now," he whispered with venom in his voice.

Scott smiled. "Don't think for a second, Phelps, that a single word you say has any effect on me. But, get this straight, you worthless waste of oxygen—I was raised to take care of my own, and if you so much as send a wrong look in Alexandra's direction, you'll wish you hadn't."

Duncan sneered and considered Scott for a moment. Just as he had done during their dinner at the hotel in Colorado, he sized up the competition and his face turned scarlet with infuriation. He couldn't win a direct confrontation with this man to save his life unless he wanted to make an all-out scene. With a glare, he turned on his heel and walked away.

Alexandra walked over to Scott as Duncan turned to leave. "Not so random question. What was *that* all about?" They watched the Zellez team walk out the door.

"I think our Duncan over there wants a showdown."

"Well I looked at the final presentation this morning and he doesn't have a prayer."

Scott smiled at her. "I'm glad we're back on the same side, Alex. It would have been lonely without you."

Chapter Eight

David looked across his desk at his two favorite employees and smiled. They sat side by side in front of him, both looking very professional and without a trace of the hostility he had initially sensed so often between them.

"I don't think I've ever seen a more brilliant piece of work in my entire career," he praised. That morning after several trial runs, Scott had finally given the last dress rehearsal of the presentation with David and Alexandra as his audience.

"Alex," David continued, "the concept and the materials are stunning. And Scott, your delivery was impeccable. I knew you two would be amazing together, but I never envisioned a presentation quite this good."

Alexandra smiled. "Gee, you think we'll win?" she asked with a wink. She had to admit—David had been right at every step along the way. He could be infuriating at times, but he was rarely wrong.

David shook his head. "Win? No. I think we'll absolutely decimate the competition."

Scott's gaze caught Alexandra's. "They don't stand a chance," he said. "Not with all the talent in this room."

David smiled and rubbed his chin with his fingers in thought. "Now that we're ready to present, you realize we're done with an entire week to spare."

"Great," Alexandra said. "Gives us all some time to catch up on the day-to-day things."

"You wish," David said with a chuckle. "Actually I just got an interesting call this morning."

Scott leaned forward. "And?" he urged, dreading from David's tone what sounded like a travel assignment in the making. Even a week apart from Alexandra was too much as far as he was concerned. But the week before their big presentation? That would be even worse somehow.

"How would the two of you feel about handling a small project for me this week? I can't think of a better team."

Alexandra shrugged. "Sure. You know we're happy to help."

David studied the two of them for a moment. Maybe it was the tone with which Alexandra had said "we," but if he didn't know better, he could have sworn he saw a spark there.

"I'm so glad to hear that. You'll both need to pack for a full five days. I'll get your itinerary to Sarah before you head to the airport tonight."

•

"Montana?" Mary would have jumped up and down were it not for the full cup of tea in her hand. "And with Scott Falconer? Oh, Alexandra, are you ever in big trouble. Big. Huge. So awesome."

Alex rolled her eyes heavenward as she tossed a skirt into the open suitcase on her bed. "Business trip, Mary. Business trip."

Her friend set her cup down on the nightstand. "Sure. Remember what happened on the last 'business trip.'"

"That was different." Alexandra fought to keep the color from rising in her face as she thought of the cabin. "I don't think we'll be running into any avalanches this time around."

Mary shook her head knowingly. "It sure was different. I'll give you that. You two went traipsing off to Colorado with just the start of an attraction there. Now you're smack dab in the middle of it. Hormones raging out of control ..."

Alexandra stopped folding her clothes and straightened her back. "I'll be strong," she said with as much sarcasm as she could muster. "But I sure wish we could have been sent somewhere sunny. I don't imagine there's much snow in the Bahamas."

Alexandra snapped her suitcase shut and pictured blue waters lined by white sand. She wouldn't admit it to her friend, but she was secretly glad that with such short notice, she and Scott had been forced to take separate flights. She remembered the tingle she felt sitting so close to him on the plane to Colorado. It was best to remove all temptation.

"Too bad you have such strange luck with each other. I'd say the Bahamas would be far too dangerous," Mary said.

"What do you mean?"

"Well, you'd probably wind up stranded together, but because of a hurricane instead of an avalanche. Or hey—how about that Bermuda Triangle? If you two were on the same flight, you'd wind up lost together there for sure. Abducted by aliens or something."

"You're nuts," Alexandra said with a laugh. Mary's logic did have a certain ring of truth to it. After all, she had been the one to rescue them from a locked supply closet not all that long ago.

With Mary safely housesitting, Alexandra left for the airport. She stopped at the office and picked up her schedule, and after looking at it, had to wonder what David had been thinking. She and Scott had possibly two days worth of work in Montana, and five full days in which to complete it.

Try as she might, the extra time they would have together was the only thing that ran through Alexandra's mind during the flight.

•

Scott met Alexandra in the hotel lobby while the valet pulled his car around. He called out, "I've got the list of property Rio Safari owns in Montana. What did David tuck into your itinerary?" He smiled as she crossed the floor to him, gliding with that feminine sway of denim moving around her hips that made him do a double-take.

"A list of the property they're interested in buying." She smoothed back a piece of auburn hair that threatened to escape her ponytail and pretended not to notice how he watched her. "What do you think he's up to?"

"David? Who knows? He's on to something, though, or he wouldn't have sent us to quietly do the legwork."

Scott closed the car door after Alexandra. She watched him walk around to the driver's side, noting how he seemed transformed by the Montana air. With his tan skin and flashing blue eyes, the sight of him after a day apart nearly made her forget why they'd come to Montana. She breathed deeply. Friendly colleagues for now. She had to cling to that mantra for the sake of her own control. Just a little bit longer, then who knew?

"I didn't realize I had a built-in chauffeur," she said, "but I guess you must know Helena pretty well."

"Well enough not to get lost. My family's ranch is just a couple hours away from here. My brothers and I used to come here sometimes shopping as kids."

"Brothers? For that matter—ranch?"

Scott stopped at a red light and grinned wickedly. "Craig, Joe and Elliot. See how much you don't know about me? I tried to tell you ..."

Alexandra felt more alive than ever, filled with the sight of him. "Maybe it was one of them with the princess in Paris, then?" So he hadn't been joking when he'd called himself a cowboy. Was there a chance he actually was?

Scott groaned with a smile. "Craig and Joe work on the ranch with Dad. Elliot does what I do—sends money home to keep the ranch up and running the way it ought to be."

That tiny furrow marked Alexandra's forehead. "Is it in trouble?"

"No. It's just that it's hard to make a living on a cattle ranch these days. The regulations are abundant, gas prices are high and cattle prices are low. Doesn't make for a glamorous existence without a little outside financial help. It's home, our family legacy, and we decided a long time ago what we'd each contribute to it."

Alexandra sat silently staring at the man next to her. Who was he? One minute, he was in a designer suit facing off against

Duncan, and the next he was wearing beat-up cowboy boots and talking about his family's ranch.

For the next several hours, they visited City Hall, a courthouse, one library and title company after title company. By the end of the day, they had all the records they could find of the property Rio Safari had acquired in the past couple of years. Ironically, the same handful of companies from which they had purchased these properties had also recently bought up all the property in which Rio was now interested.

"Don't you think this is strange?" Alexandra asked Scott as she flipped through the papers.

"Feels a little off—especially since all these companies are set up anonymously with an agent as the contact."

"All of them. I noticed that. I wonder if it's the same person behind all these companies?"

Scott shrugged. "Maybe David can shed some light when we go back. He didn't seem to want us to dig any deeper right now."

Alexandra settled into her seat as Scott drove them back to their hotel. "Did you see when our return flights were scheduled for?"

Scott nodded. "Yup. Friday. David wrote on the bottom of my itinerary that I'm to take the next three days off and that he doesn't want to see me until after the presentation."

"Wrote the same thing on mine," Alexandra added.

Scott stopped at a red light. "Let's check out of the hotel tonight, Alex. Let's not stay there."

"Got a better place in mind?" She certainly hoped he did. With all the time David had given them to spare, they might as well sleep somewhere interesting.

"A much better one, in fact. A place I'm dying to show you." He placed his hand over his heart and sighed as he watched her run to gather her luggage.

An hour later, Alexandra found herself seated beside Scott, well into the long drive to his family's ranch. "I can't believe I let you talk me into this," she said in a tone of amazement.

"I can't believe you let me, either," he chided. Did he dare to hope she was rethinking her argument against having a relationship with him?

"Random question. Do you like barbecue?"

"Does anyone *not*?" She punched him lightly on the arm. "So there are guest rooms?"

"My father lives in the main house. You can stay in the extra room there. Craig works as foreman now, so he and his wife built their own house across the hill from Dad's place."

"What about Joe?"

"Joe? He's younger than me by a few years and not even dating anyone seriously. No need for a place of his own, so he still stays at Dad's."

"Where are you going to sleep?" Alexandra asked, hoping not to sound too obvious in her concern.

"I'll stay with Craig and Emma. They have a spare room, at least until the baby comes. Why? Worried?"

She was worried, though she refused to admit it. Every time she closed her eyes at night, the remembrance of Scott's touches in the cabin sprang back into her mind. It was as if the sensation itself lingered on her skin.

After driving for some miles on a small, paved road, they turned onto a large gravel road, then onto a smaller dirt road, and finally onto what Alexandra declared had to be a glorified trail worn by some kind of animal.

"How far to the ranch?" she asked.

"Oh, we've been on it for the last few miles."

As their car bounced along the rutted trail toward the mountains, a large log home that looked like a miniature resort came into view.

"To your left is Craig's place," Scott explained in his best tour guide voice. "Around and to the front you will find many, many mountains, and if you look to the west just over them, a glorious sunset." He gestured in the other direction. "To your right please notice under all that snow, a group of rare alfalfa fields, once thought by city dwellers to be mythical creatures, much like ranchers."

He smiled at her and continued. "At last we come upon the highlight of our tour, the main house." Scott pulled the car into the driveway and turned off the engine in front of an older though well-maintained log house with a red metal roof. Pole fences surrounded the yards of the houses and perfectly tightened barbed wire fences sectioned off the fields. Behind the main house, the road disappeared into a canyon in the mountains.

Alexandra spotted an entire orchard covered in snow, frosty signs pointing to an enormous vegetable garden, and a pond with an icicle-ornamented creek flowing through it. She could imagine how the place must look in the springtime with wildflowers covering the hillsides and fresh green grass lining the banks of the pond. The place was a fantasy world all its own.

Alexandra looked at Scott as the colors of the sunset fell across his face. "So this is where all your extra money goes." She had never admired him so much as she did right then. To think she'd ever listened to Sarah's ridiculous stories, or compared this beautiful man to someone like D— *Bleh.* She couldn't even finish her name in her head. It gave her the shivers to think how badly she'd misjudged him at first.

He nodded. "This is where the money goes. No investment like it in the world."

She held his gaze with hers as he leaned closer to her, close enough to be dangerous, close enough to shatter the co-worker boundaries she'd been so careful to rebuild this near to the presentation day ahead. Just as his lips threatened to take hers in another kiss, the sound of a door opening jolted them apart.

"Scott? What on earth are you doing here? We weren't expecting you for another couple weeks." Scott's father, followed by the rest of the family, ran down the porch stairs and over to the car.

"Look, Mr. Antisocial has a girlfriend with him," one of them said. It sent a little rush of warmth through Alexandra to hear Scott called that. And to hear herself called *that.*

Scott greeted them with bear hugs. "Joe," he said to the one who had made the girlfriend comment, "this is Alexandra. She's a colleague from work."

"Sure she is," Joe said knowingly while shaking Alexandra's hand. She was surprised how closely he resembled Scott, though his brown eyes and carefree demeanor set him completely apart from his older brother. "Craig's standing up to his knees in snow, but he's got some BBQ going in the backyard for dinner. And Emma's got some killer peach pie to go with it. You're just in time."

Scott introduced her to the rest of the family and then walked with her up to the guestroom.

"Joe's been staying with Craig. I just finished repainting his room," his father called out up the stairs after them. "One of you can have the guestroom and the other gets Joe's old room here. Just don't touch the walls."

Scott smiled at her sweetly. "Does this arrangement work for you? I know I promised to keep a lot of space between our sleeping arrangements."

"It's wonderful. This place seems like paradise compared to where I live now. And I'm sure we'll somehow find a way to control ourselves."

He ignored her sarcasm. "This place sure knocks all the rumors about Paris, movie stars and princesses right out of the water, doesn't it?" he asked.

"As if I ever believed any of that."

With snow still on the ground around the barbecue grill, Craig brought the meal inside to eat at the kitchen table. They were a lively, happy bunch who laughed, ate and then headed for bed as soon as the light was gone. Everything seemed very straightforward with none of the insane competition and constant looking over the shoulder that happened so persistently in big business. Alexandra smiled and helped herself to a piece of pie.

"Got to get up and feed the cattle early," a very pregnant Emma explained as they all left the kitchen.

Alexandra followed their example and went upstairs with

Scott leading the way. She took a hot bath and fell asleep the second her head hit the soft pillow. She had traveled too many hours and felt completely safe on the ranch with Scott and his family. The combination lulled her to sleep immediately. She smiled as she thought of Scott in the next room. Maybe she'd resisted something very special for all the wrong reasons. Maybe Scott had been right about acting on their feelings all along. After the presentation ...

In the middle of the night, Alexandra awoke and felt her way to the bathroom. There were no streetlights, no nightlights, and not even a sliver of moonlight coming through the closed curtains to guide the way. This far in the country, nighttime was really and truly dark. All she could see outside through a distant window down the hall was a blanket of endless stars sparkling against a black backdrop of sky.

She may as well have been walking with her eyes shut as she made her way back to her room. Running her hand along the wall, she finally found the doorknob and slid into her nice, warm bed.

•

Alexandra awoke under a stream of sunshine the next morning. She covered her head with a pillow. There was no point in denying it. She was hopelessly, stupidly, unquestionably falling in love with Scott Falconer.

"You idiot," Alexandra said out loud to herself. "Whatever happened to 'never date a colleague' and 'listen to your head not your heart'?" Mary had been right all along in her suspicions. After the presentation, she'd tell Scott how she felt. She could trust him. She knew she could. And if she ever had a doubt, she'd simply keep her promise to give him a chance to prove himself to her.

Scott knocked on her door, interrupting a good solid stretch. "Are you decent?" he whispered loudly.

"No." She laughed.

He opened the door and walked into the room. He had already showered and shaved, and already had his first morning cup of coffee in his hand. He looked less like a colleague and more like a part of her life with each passing day.

"What's this about the head and heart?"

"Eavesdropper."

He shrugged. "It always seemed to me that when people know in their heads that someone is wrong for them, but get carried away by their hearts, they end up in trouble. And when they go for someone who looks right on paper—in their heads—but the emotion isn't there in the heart, that's just as bad."

"So you're saying don't get involved unless the head and the heart line up?"

"Exactly."

Alexandra smiled at him brightly through tufts of disheveled hair. Why hadn't she realized it this solidly before? All the while, he had stood in front of her professing his feelings while she had held him away at a safe, business-like distance. Never once had she realized that she couldn't imagine going back to her life or to her office without him there. And never once had she realized he'd meant what he'd said to her. How could she have ever thought a woman like the sub-zero Mac Stevens could hold his heart? She loved the corporate version of Scott Falconer, and she loved the cowboy she'd just discovered in him.

"All right, then," he said with a perplexed look on his face, "get dressed. We've got cows to feed."

•

As the tractor bounced slowly over lumps in the frozen field, Alexandra knew she had the easy part of the job. She sat bundled up in the heated cab of the tractor with Scott's father and watched the herd trot expectantly toward the wagon full of hay that they pulled behind. She couldn't imagine a situation any further from her tailored suits and leather executive chair.

Every once in a while, she caught sight of a pile of hay flying off to the side of the wagon, but the stack rose too high for Alexandra to see anything but hay bales out the back window. She wished she could watch Scott pull the bales down, cut the twine and feed the hay off the edge of the wagon. She remembered the long underwear top he'd worn in the cabin as he tossed wood onto the fire. He must be wearing that underneath his heavy coat, she mused. She couldn't see him, no matter which way she turned the mirror.

Scott's father smiled at Alexandra as the tractor crept along the field. He slowly brought the vehicle to a stop and turned to her.

From far back on the wagon, Scott banged on something metal. "What's going on?" he called.

Mr. Falconer nodded toward the door of the tractor. "Go on," he told Alexandra, "get out and climb up on the wagon. Looks like you're dyin' to."

Alexandra didn't have to be told twice. Scott's smile shot a sensation through to her toes as his gloved hand caught hers and pulled her up onto the wagon with him. Hay dust coated his long eyelashes, and somehow made his blue eyes bluer.

"Here," he said as he kicked over a pile of orange twine, "you can untangle and roll this stuff up as I cut it off the bales."

Scott smiled again when Alexandra didn't so much as flinch at the dirt and the hay around her, and immediately started rolling the twine up neatly. She bet Mackenzie wouldn't have gone near a hay wagon.

"Giving the city girl something productive to do, huh?" Up until now, Alexandra had assumed this way of life was either long gone or something just told about in stories. But here it was, alive in Scott Falconer. He really hadn't been kidding when he'd said he was a cowboy.

Alexandra's laughing voice pulled Scott from his thoughts and he swung a pile of hay wide out into the field. "What do you think David or Sarah would say if they could see us now?" He laughed and his breath was frosty in the morning air.

"I think they'd believe we're a couple," Alexandra said quietly. "Mary does."

Scott paused for a moment and watched Alexandra's face turn red. "Or that we just want very, very much to be," he whispered.

Alexandra's heart pounded under her layers of clothing. The intensity in Scott's eyes, the scent of his body mingled with the fresh hay, the pure masculinity he exuded as he lifted each hundred-pound bale with ease—these things wore very effectively on her self-restraint.

"I'm sorry," she began. "I'm not being very professional here."

"It's about time," he answered with a grin.

"I'm curious what David plans to do with all the information we dug up," Alexandra said, trying to steer the conversation back to safer territory.

Scott kicked the last bit of hay over the side of the wagon and sat down next to her. "Do you really want to talk business, Alex?"

"Until after the presentation, that's the only subject for us. It's too important."

She gripped the bundle of baler twine as tightly now as she had the surprise cabin arrangements during their flight to Colorado.

"So what happens after the presentation, Alex?"

"I guess you'll have to wait and see," she teased. She hadn't truly known what she would say to him after the presentation until just that morning. Now her intentions had changed. She wanted to be with this man even if it took all her courage. She drew in a shaky breath.

Scott laughed out loud. "Who would have thought there was a blatant flirt hidden behind the businesswoman exterior?"

"Probably the same person who would have thought there was a bona fide cattle rancher lurking under those three-thousand-dollar suits."

Scott's father rolled the tractor up into the yard and jumped out. "Craig and Joe can reload the wagon for tomorrow's feeding. I'll be doin' some woodworking in the shed if you need me. Don't catch cold." The older man gave the two of them a knowing glance before walking away, not that they ever looked away from each other long enough to notice.

They walked into the house and a few minutes later,

Alexandra sat cross-legged in front of the fireplace, pulling first one photo album and then another into her lap. Scott's whole life was open to her as she saw picture after picture of the baby becoming a boy, and the boy becoming a man.

Scott emerged from the kitchen with two steaming mugs of hot chocolate. "Oh, no." He winced visibly. "Bare bottoms and bear skin rugs."

"I was thinking of swiping a couple of these for the break room bulletin board."

Alexandra's hair cascaded loosely down her back, glowing warmly in the firelight. Scott could imagine her with him like this forever. She fit so naturally into his life without even trying. Alexandra challenged him in the office and complemented him in this place so far removed from it. He ached for her. He'd never ached for anyone before.

"I wish I could have met your mother while she was alive," she said, "She must have been an amazing person."

"She was."

"And I can't believe how cute you were as a child. The girls must have run wild after you in school." She flipped another page over.

Alexandra looked up from the photo album when Scott didn't say anything. The bare desire in his eyes reached her immediately and she drew in a quick breath as his mere expression uncoiled her own desire deep within her.

Scott set down the hot chocolate and closed the distance between him and Alexandra in a single step. He dropped on his knees to the floor and twined his hands into her hair.

She rose to her own knees, pressing closer to him as he kissed her softly.

"What have you done to me?" Scott ran his hands violently through his own dark hair and gave a little laugh. Frustration glittered somewhere in his eyes. "I had more control when I was the walking teenage hormone you saw in those pictures."

With a trembling hand, Alexandra picked up the photo album she had been begun looking through. As she moved to put it back in its place, a single photo slid from its pages and dropped to the floor. She knew its subject all too well and it froze her.

Scott took the picture from her shaking fingers and saw the image of his own smiling face and his arm around Mac Stevens. He didn't even remember where they'd taken that picture, nor did he care.

Alexandra whispered the first thing she thought. "What do you feel when you see Mac Stevens?"

"Nothing good. Nothing at all really." He flung the picture into the fire and watched the flames curl around the paper and obliterate the memory captured there. "Nothing like what I feel when I see you."

His blue eyes were dark with emotion and Alexandra put her fingers up to his lips.

"That was *not* a sign," he said.

"But, we keep coming back to the same issue. We're colleagues working together on an important presentation. I admit everything has changed, but I really think we ought to wait and talk about this subject after the presentation when there isn't so much money at stake for so many people. We just need to focus a little bit longer."

"I hate this, you know."

"Me, too."

Chapter Nine

Alexandra awoke the next morning with a long, cat-like stretch and looked at the clock. Why hadn't anyone gotten her up in time to help feed the cattle? Not that she'd been much help the last time, but she couldn't let a chance to sit on the back of a hay wagon with Scott pass her by. She jumped out of bed, took a quick shower and ran downstairs. From the silence in the house, she knew she was already too late.

Scott sat in the kitchen with a pile of business magazines and paperwork scattered out on the table. "Hi." He smiled broadly.

"Why didn't you wake me up?"

"I thought I'd let you sleep in. We have hired hands come help out a few times a week, and they took care of feeding today. Dad and the rest of the gang left for town a few minutes ago. I have the distinct impression they're trying to give us some privacy." He smiled at her over his cup of coffee.

At least she hadn't missed anything. Alexandra poured her own cup and sat down next to him. He hadn't shaven again, she noticed. She hadn't seen him like that since they were stuck in the cabin together. Scott seemed so potently male with his stubble and denim shirt. She noticed his well-manicured hands and perfectly trimmed hair, which somehow seemed to complement his rugged look instead of clashing with it. He was a contradiction sometimes—one she couldn't stop trying to figure out.

"What are you working on?" she finally asked.

He looked up from his spreadsheets to her face, fresh and bright with the morning. This was an Alexandra Hunter he would have hardly recognized not long ago. She was well-rested, relaxed, and looking at him with an expression of open interest in her eyes.

"I'm thinking about putting together a business plan," he answered. "There's a thousand-acre chunk of land that backs up to our fence line just over the hill."

"You need more land?" The ranch already seemed huge to her as it was.

"We might." Scott looked at her for a moment as if debating letting her in on a secret mission. "See, Elliot and his wife are thinking of coming back from New York. They don't want to raise a family in the city. Can't say that I blame them."

"So he wants to expand the ranch?"

"Well, we don't have enough rangeland to run enough additional cattle—we wouldn't even with that new piece. But, if Elliot gives up his cushy, six-figure job to move back, we'll need to come up with some other way to generate a lot of extra income here." He held up a handful of flyers and a spreadsheet filled with pencil marks.

Alexandra loved watching him work his magic with numbers as he added up columns in his head. A calculator sat on the edge of the table, but he never seemed to think to reach for it.

"So what have you come up with?" she asked.

"A working dude ranch." He grinned. "I think we can make it pay off."

Alexandra laughed. "Okay, Tom Sawyer."

Scott shot her an intrigued look.

"It's like the white-washed fence story," she said. "People will actually pay you to come out and experience ranch life because it's a novelty for them. They'll pay you while you 'let' them do your chores. And they'll get a huge kick out of doing them." She shook her head and took a sip of coffee. "You'll make money hand over fist."

"Then it must be a good idea, huh?" He stacked the papers

neatly into a single pile and dropped his pencil on top.

Alexandra nodded. "I think it's brilliant." She propped herself up on her elbow and smiled at him again. She couldn't remember ever feeling so good in the morning. "The land is so amazing, how could anyone pass up seeing it—even if only for a week or two? So what would you build on the extra thousand acres?"

"There's a pretty little meadow right on the edge of it. We could build five or six small log cabins there. It's mostly timberland up behind the meadow, so we could mark out horse riding trails, hiking trails—who knows? We could even put in a fishing pond or another swimming hole or something. And barbecue pits to go with the picnic area. Craig would never let me hear the end of it if we didn't barbecue something for the visitors."

"It sounds like so much fun. I'll be your first guest when you open for business." She took a sip of her coffee. "I can just imagine all the exciting things you'll do with it."

"Have you ever thought of leaving corporate life, Alex?"

"I really hadn't," she said softly. "But I have to admit that after seeing this place, the view of downtown Seattle from my office window hardly seems as appealing. I look at this place and I think I've been stuck in a rut my entire life and I didn't even know it."

Scott leaned back in his chair and stretched his long legs out under the table. "To tell you the truth, Chicago isn't that appealing either. Never has been. I love numbers, business, my family and this land. The rest is just a means to an end."

"You're saying you'd do what Elliot is going to do?"

"Maybe someday. When I have a reason to." He leaned forward. "But enough of that. We've got a bottle baby to feed."

"A bottle baby?"

"I'll introduce you to him in a minute. I'd better get his breakfast ready first."

Alexandra watched as Scott went to the sink and mixed some special powdered milk up in a bowl with warm water. He poured about a quart of the liquid into a large bottle and pulled a giant rubber nipple over the top of it.

Scott took Alexandra by the hand and grinned as he led her to the barn. As they neared a pen, a shiny little black nose poked out from between the boards.

"This is Huey," Scott said. "His mother disappeared this winter. I think he's more pig than calf from the way he goes through bottles."

Alexandra reached her hand through the panels and gently touched the curly top of the calf's head. Its soft, white hair tickled her fingers as she petted the little animal. "I've never seen anything so sweet."

"They always look cute and clean when they're babies. Wait until he gets bigger. Then it'll be a whole 'nother story,"

"Can I try?" Alexandra asked.

Scott put the big bottle into her smaller, feminine hands. "Hold onto the bottle like this." He moved close to her, feeling the heat from her body as he wrapped his arms around her. "He'll pull the top off if you're not careful."

Alexandra lowered the bottle between the boards and laughed when the little calf nudged it hard. His big, brown eyes rolled back as he greedily gulped down the warm liquid. Happy to be fed, his tail swung side to side almost like a puppy's.

Scott leaned close to Alexandra's ear and said, "Pull it back for a second and let some air in the bottle."

Chills swept through Alexandra's body at the nearness of Scott's lips to her neck and ears. He hadn't touched her when he spoke, but the thought of him so close to her had nearly the same effect. Just as she had been attracted to his suave businessman charm the minute she first saw him on the freeway, now her heart pounded at the rugged strength she saw in him here. He was the best of both worlds, and the careful touch of his hand on hers was driving her wild.

When the calf drained the bottle, she turned to Scott. "What do I do next?"

"You kiss me?"

She felt the calf tug on the tail of her shirt through the boards, leaving a glob of milk slobber there. Alexandra made a little noise. "Yuck. Drool."

Scott pulled away from her. "Come on. I don't kiss that badly."

Alexandra giggled. "Enough already," she half-laughed. "We're crossing that line again." Yet she wanted to keep crossing it.

Scott stepped away from her reluctantly. "I guess that brings us back to a thrilling choice of chores or office talk."

"Or," she said with a suggestive laugh, "we could forget about talking at all and see if the ice on your pond is thick enough to hold up a couple of ice-skaters."

Scott grinned broadly as childhood memories with his brothers rushed back to him. "I can show you an even better twist on that idea."

Intrigued, Alexandra picked up the fallen milk bottle and carried it back into the house. She grabbed a dry pair of gloves and a thicker scarf. "I'm ready," she declared.

Scott zipped his coat up to his throat and led her down a bank into a field. He pushed aside a bunch of cold, brown willow limbs and ushered Alexandra down into the wide ditch that twisted through the property.

"There was always too much snow on top of the ice on the pond. So, Craig, Joe, Elliot and I would come here instead. There's enough brush lining the sides of the ditch to hold out a little of the white stuff. We don't even need ice skates."

Alexandra grabbed his gloved hand to steady herself as she stepped out onto the slick surface. "How deep is the water under us?" she asked.

"Only a foot or so. That's another bonus. No messy, irritating drownings."

For once, in how many years she couldn't imagine, not a single thought of the office weighed on Alexandra Hunter. She felt like a little girl and a woman rolled into one. There were no nagging feelings about some task left undone at work. She didn't feel the need to strap her cell phone onto her belt or log in to check her e-mail. She was free with Scott Falconer, loved the way she felt near him, loved the way he smiled at her ...

"Come on," he yelled as he started to run on the slippery surface.

Alexandra planted her feet firmly on the ice and moved her legs almost as if she were cross-country skiing. Faster and faster she ran across the ice, but try as she might, Scott's long, muscular legs carried him a few yards beyond catching up to him.

As she ran, she crossed over fluffy bunches of cream-colored stuff where the velvety brown cattails had broken open along the banks. The slick ice took on a light greenish tone under her feet, and here and there she had to dodge a hard brown lump where a rock poked through.

"Wait, wait," she cried out with a laugh and stopped to catch her breath.

Scott circled back to her. The crisp air stained his cheeks with hint of red and added a sparkle to his stunning blue eyes. "You've been behind a computer for too long. Getting soft."

"I'll show you soft," she teased as she cut in front of him to throw him off balance. In a flash, she was off ahead of Scott, leaving him to watch her in amazement. Just as she had been surprised to find a rancher lurking behind his corporate image, he couldn't believe who he had discovered hiding behind hers. This woman racing ahead of him on the ice seemed to fit with ease into the strange mixture of his life. He would never have guessed it that day on the freeway. He'd never known a woman accustomed to silk who seemed to thrive out in the middle of nowhere surrounded by broken cattails and calf slobber.

"You cheat!" Scott caught up with her after a minute. "Wait up a second. I forgot to mention something," he said as he gazed down in to her shining, emerald eyes. "Damn if just looking at you isn't going to be my undoing." When Alexandra looked startled, Scott realized he had spoken his thought aloud. He certainly hadn't meant to.

"That's what you forgot to mention?"

His voice deepened. "A little more than an hour away from here, there's going to be an area get-together tonight."

"A get-together?"

"We have the same one every year just before the holidays. The whole party is held in the middle of a field outside town. There's usually a big bonfire, food set up on all the tailgates. They string Christmas lights up along the fences. A stage is set up with a different band every year so people can dance. People line up different craft booths along the edges. It looks a little like a holiday carnival."

"It sounds fun. I haven't been to something like that in—ever."

"I know it's no ritzy Rio Safari gala, but I thought you might like to go with me. With us, I mean—the whole family's going."

Alexandra smiled to herself. She'd already had the chance to watch Scott don a tuxedo and mingle with the elite. He'd ballroom danced, sipped champagne, courted clients and sat through a long night with her in the emergency room. Still, she wondered how he'd look in jeans and a sweater doing some sort of country dancing by bonfire light. The image seemed simple enough, but Alexandra thought it might be fun to guess which world Scott Falconer fit into better—corporate or countryside. Would she be able to tell?

She only said, "I wouldn't miss it for the world."

•

Alexandra and the entire Falconer family piled into a big Suburban just as the sunlight started to fade, and bounced along for well over an hour until the glow of an enormous bonfire came into view. She suspected they were closer to Helena again than they were to the ranch, but this far out in the country at night, she couldn't tell for sure.

Alexandra sat behind Mr. Falconer as he drove. From her position, she could watch Scott sitting in the passenger seat talking and laughing with his father. She almost laughed out loud as she remembered everything Sarah had told her that first day she'd met Scott. She'd pegged him as a shiftless, spoiled rich guy. He'd turned out to be a hardworking executive and cowboy rolled into one. She'd thought he was a playboy, but he had shown her a respect for her values and genuinely seemed to be looking for a commitment. Was it any wonder her initial butterflies had evolved into a powerful longing?

Under the illumination of Christmas lights and the bonfire, Alexandra could see the gathering of people was far bigger than she had imagined. The scene she was looking at was more like a small state fair—without the carnival rides—all centered around the biggest bonfire she'd ever seen. A dozen children giggled and thrust marshmallows and hotdogs on spikes wherever they could find an open space along the bottom of the teepee of burning wood.

A large area had been plowed out for the event, but along the edges of that area, people ran out into the blackness of the night to throw snowballs at each other. They were nearly impossible to see, but their mock war cries carried far across the countryside. Starlight hit the snow-covered mountains far in the distance and bounced delicately off their white caps.

And the smells of food cooking were heavenly. One of the vendors who had set up a large corner booth had rows of barbecued ribs turning over a spit. He slathered on more sauce as he turned the meat over to let it sizzle from a new angle. Another booth served large foam cups full of hot, steaming apple cider and other drinks. Alexandra saw caramel-covered apples, pots of homemade chili, hot deli sandwiches—the possibilities were endless.

Scott took Alexandra by the hand and led her down the tantalizing row of food booths, past the tables of fudge and mincemeat pies to the start of the row of crafts tables.

"Dad always buys one new stained glass Christmas tree ornament here every year from Mrs. Smith. She makes them by hand. Her husband does all that woodcarving on the table over here. I think they must work all year just to have enough on hand for this festival."

Scott gestured and led Alexandra over to a table stacked with hand-carved jewelry boxes and wooden signs decorated with elk and bear. She picked up a small, cream-colored wooden box, opened the lid and breathed in deeply. The earthy, rich scent of the wood filled her senses.

"This is beautiful wood," she said to the tall, blond man behind the table. "It almost smells like cedar, but not quite. What is it?"

"Juniper. Now if we could just find some use for all the sagebrush we have around here, we'd be set for life."

Alexandra laughed and walked on with Scott, "Thank you for bringing me here."

"This was the place to be when I was in school." Scott nodded to a group of teenagers swarming all over the backs of several pickup trucks. "It you didn't make it to this, you just weren't with it. Things around here don't change much." They strolled past a bunch of welded iron sculptures.

"It's definitely not like things back in the office, is it? Things are changing just about every minute back there." She picked up a self-published cookbook of recipes used on the Oregon Trail and put it back down again. "I can't even remember when I last cooked a full meal. There's never any time."

"That's why I like it here," he said. "The pace gives a person time to think, time to run deeper instead of faster. Not that the ranch isn't a lot of hard work, though."

"Well, I wasn't raised anywhere so glamorous as this," she teased. "I'm just a girl who wound up in the 'burbs, got bounced around between foster homes, then made it to college and moved into the city to work."

"How did they die?"

She shrugged. "Car accident on bad roads. Happens everyday. I wonder all the time what life would have been like with a real family."

"You ought to be proud of what you've done on your own. But don't you ever think of adding just a little bit more?"

They teetered too close to crossing that personal line into romantic taboo again. "I thought that's what I was doing right now." She had an impossible time acting like the friendly colleague she was supposed to be.

Scott grinned at her as she stood facing him with her arms crossed in front of her chest. Her breath hung frosty in the air and she looked at him as if she expected him to say something meaningful in response. But how could he? All he could think of was the way the cold air added a shine to her green eyes and a kiss of stained crimson to her cheeks.

After a long pause he said softly, "Are you too cold? We could get back closer to the fire."

"I'm doing fine, but I think we've almost seen all there is to see, and done all there is to do here." The twinkle in his eyes and the colored glow of Christmas lights on his face had taken all her focus away from the festival as it was. She'd have been happy huddled in a cave with him at that moment.

Scott's attention slipped briefly away from her gaze and excitement leapt into his voice. "Do you hear that?" he asked. "The band's going to start. Come on." He grabbed her hand firmly and tugged. "This is the best part."

Alexandra nearly had to run to keep from being dragged. "Slow down a little."

"You don't want to dance?" His tone of disbelief told her that not wanting to dance was no better than a crime.

"If it's some kind of country swing, square dancing, polka thing—then, no thanks. I'll just stand on the sidelines and watch you."

Scott laughed at her. "You've been sheltered in the city way, way too long. We're not a bunch of rednecks out here, you know."

Joe sauntered past them, surrounded by a group of friends. "Hey, big brother. Tell Dad I'm going night skiing. The guys will give me a lift home in the morning. You know, the usual ritual."

"Sure. I remember the routine," Scott said as he turned back to Alexandra. "He does this every year. I'm afraid he's never going to grow up. Wonder which bone he'll break this year. The stories I could tell." He waved his hand in a dismissive motion.

"Now let's dance!"

With a burst of energy, Scott swung Alexandra around and whirled her into the crowd. The first beats of a solid rock and roll song filled the night. This was better than a nightclub, Alexandra thought as they danced together. They laughed and moved faster, swaying and bouncing energetically to the rhythm of the guitar and the beat of a drum. All of the visitors to the festival filtered in from the craft tables and food booths, some running, others walking hand-in-hand to join in what was obviously an event they looked forward to each year. Scott and Alexandra were forced closer together as the area around the bonfire and in front of the band grew more and more crowded.

A subtle night breeze flowed across the group of people and pushed feathery clouds over the bright stars overhead. Then the opening song ended with a drumbeat and the band began playing the first notes of a slow, romantic ballad that Alexandra remembered from college. Scott pulled Alexandra against his chest without missing a note. "Having fun?"

"Tons," she answered as she looked up at the sparkling blanket of stars coating the night sky. "My friends and I used to dance to this song way back in the day, before I'd even taken my first job."

He rested his cheek against her hair briefly and then thought better of it. "You're not even thirty yet, and you're talking like you're a hundred years old."

He couldn't have wished for a warmer, more beautiful woman in his arms. He smiled, knowing he knew another Alexandra —the sleek, commanding marketing executive who could slip back into a designer suit and charm a room with the snap of a briefcase lock. With her faded jeans and ponytailed hair, no one in the Falconer family had believed him at first when he told them of Alexandra's cool, in-control reputation. After getting to know her, he could barely believe it himself.

"The stars remind me of something Joe and I used to do," Scott said quietly with a hint of nostalgia in his voice.

"Something even better than skating down the ditch? Or

getting covered in hay dust?"

"Wouldn't think it possible, would you?" He laughed and continued, "Sometimes when the ranch hands got sidetracked, they'd leave a hay wagon only partially loaded. When they left to take care of whatever emergency had hit, they pulled a heavy black tarp over what few hay bales they'd already loaded. Joe and I would slip underneath the tarp and lay down between bales. It was pitch black under there except for the hundreds of tiny, pinprick holes that the sharp hay had poked in the plastic. We would stay there for the longest time just looking up. With the sun shining down on the tarp and those tiny holes, it looked exactly like we were seeing a night sky full of brand new stars and constellations that no one had ever seen before. And with the smell of the hay, it was magical."

Alexandra could nearly feel the sensations. "That must have been wonderful. But what if some of the hay had fallen? You two could have been squashed under there."

"Nah. We were a bunch of little monkeys crawling all over the place. Never in any danger I don't think. We climbed trees, swam in the pond—pretty much ran wild through the hills. I don't think there's an inch of land on the ranch I haven't walked across."

Craig and Emma danced slowly over to them, held far apart by Emma's rounded belly. "We don't mean to interrupt," Craig said, "but Em and I are going to get a hotel in town. She's getting too tired to bounce back home on those dirt roads tonight. The baby isn't up for that kind of ride at the moment. He's kicking like crazy."

"Did you let Dad know you aren't riding back with us?" Scott asked.

"Sure did. But he said something about a poker game tonight, so I don't know what he's got figured for transportation back. We'll work it out in the morning I guess."

They walked away as the ballad ended. "So much for having chaperones with us. Does your family always disappear on you like that?" Alexandra asked.

"During this celebration? We usually do spend a little of it together. I hate to give up the dancing, but I think we'd better track down Dad before he disappears into that poker game."

With mugs of hot buttered rum and apple cider in hand, they set off to locate Scott's father in the crowd. As Alexandra held onto Scott's arm, the expressions of the women around the bonfire weren't lost on her. Scott led her through the throng of visitors while the females in their path either stepped closer hoping to bump into him, or batted their eyelashes from a distance like mock southern belles. Alexandra half expected one of them to swoon. Oblivious to the reaction he caused, Scott easily spotted his father leaning against the bumper of a truck, surrounded by a group of ranchers embroiled in a lively political debate.

"Scott," he called out. "We've decided to head out to an all-night card game here in a few minutes." He smiled at Alexandra. "You'd be a fool to join us. Just us old guys and we're no fun at all." He tossed the keys to the Suburban to Scott. "Drive careful."

"You do realize Alex and I are leaving tomorrow, don't you?" Scott asked suspiciously. The smell of a setup was in the air.

"Yup," the older man acknowledged. "Enjoy the quiet time at the house while you can. And don't worry about what I'll do. I've got a ride lined up for Craig, Emma and me. Joe's on his own, though. If you see him before you leave, I found his coffee thermos left behind in the rig. He might want it if he's out in the snow for long."

Scott said goodbye to his father and walked for a while in silence with Alexandra. He hated to break the magical spell this evening had cast, but someone had to say the words. "Things seem to be winding down some. Did we miss anything or would you rather head on back?"

Alexandra looked at her watch. "It really is getting late, Scott. Maybe we'd better head back to the ranch—though I sense a family conspiracy." For the first time, she wondered exactly what Scott had told his father and brothers about her and grimaced. What they imagined about her relationship with

Scott, she could only guess.

"The conspiracy theory crossed my mine, too. Dad means well."

"I guess I must look pretty good compared to Mac Stevens."

"Alex, you look good compared to everyone."

Scott ran his fingers through the soft hair at her temples and gazed into her eyes. Then he opened the car door and helped her inside.

Chapter Ten

Night had long since fallen by the time Scott and Alexandra pulled up in front of the house. To Alexandra's chagrin, she'd fallen asleep somewhere along the way and awoke with a start when the sound of the engine stopped. An empty thermos rolled back and forth on the floor between her feet. The last thing she remembered was how strange the coffee she'd been drinking had tasted. That Joe shouldn't be allowed near a coffee pot, she thought as she pulled herself upright in the seat.

"You snore."

She yawned and looked at Scott for a few seconds. "Are you always this obnoxious when you're tired?" She leaned back against the door languidly and looked at him a little longer this time.

"You drool, too."

She could see in the blurry dashboard lights that he was trying desperately not to laugh. "You're rotten, you corporate cowboy, you."

"Maybe. But mostly I'm hungry again." He looked at her strangely. She seemed a little more than groggy, but maybe she was just truly that tired. After all, he'd never seen her completely exhausted before. He hopped out of the vehicle and walked around to open Alexandra's door. "Wasn't there some of Emma's pie or something left?" he asked.

"Dunno. But lets eat lots of it," she said. The winter air had fallen beyond crisp in the darkness. Alexandra rubbed her hands together and raced inside with her breath hanging frozen in the air around her. Scott ran ahead and stoked up the fire as she took off her coat and boots and sank down on the floor in front of it.

"It'll be roaring again in just a few minutes," he called down to her as he walked up the stairs.

Alexandra had known before what she was coming back to, but she was suddenly aware of how quiet the house was and how very far away they were from another living soul. She giggled to herself. This was a far cry from the nights when she sat alone in the office finishing up one report or another. No matter how abandoned the office got, she could still hear the hum of cars outside or office machines buzzing somewhere down the hall. That scene seemed just a shade pathetic, now that she thought about it. But this—this was different. She was far away on a ranch in pure isolation with Scott Falconer. The water cooler gang would never forget it if they ever caught wind of this, but she didn't care.

She stretched out her hands high over her head and turned toward Scott as he came back down the stairs toward her. He had tossed aside his coat and sweater. The problem was, he hadn't put on the T-shirt he held wadded up in his hand. Alexandra suspected her legs had gone weak even though she wasn't standing up. What was wrong with her? She felt warm, content, and just a little bit silly.

"Are you okay, Alex?"

"I feel great," she answered with a lopsided grin. Her gaze ran down his broad chest to his flat, hard stomach … "I'm not the crazy cat lady."

"You didn't have anything to drink, did you?" He narrowed his eyes at her. She wasn't out-of-her-head drunk, but she certainly seemed relaxed in a slightly unnatural way.

"I just had a sip or two of your buttered rum a couple hours ago. Oh, and then the coffee on the way home."

"Coffee?"

"Yeah. From that thermos Joe left in the Suburban. It was

very thoughtful of him to leave us some coffee to help us stay awake on the drive home."

"Thoughtful? Not Joe. I don't think that was just coffee in that thermos, Alex. I imagine it was laced with something he brewed on his own." No wonder his brother had run smack into the middle of a tree during last year's night skiing adventure. He and his friends acted like complete idiots on an annual basis it seemed. "You're not going blind or anything are you? I don't know if D. W. Songstram's insurance policy would cover that."

"Well, that would explain a few things, wouldn't it?" She smiled in a way she hoped was charming—it was hard to tell at the moment. "But no, my eyesight seems to be working perfectly. In fact, I'm having a really nice time using it."

Scott pulled his T-shirt down over his head and sat beside her. "You seem like you'll live."

"I'm a grown woman, Scott. Granted, I don't usually drink, but this won't be the end of me. Just don't tell David. I'm still thinking clearly, I think. I'm thinking. I ..." She studied his bottom lip for a while. Why did he have to be so delicious and so off limits?

The coffee wouldn't be the end of her, but it could very well be the end of him. Scott responded instantly to the look in Alexandra's eyes.

He stood suddenly. "Want some pie?" Tea, cake, anything to get him out of the room and away from her for a few minutes ...

She nodded eagerly as he walked into the kitchen. Emma's peach pie was divine and she thought it best to get some food into her empty stomach. She didn't know what Joe had added to that coffee, but she'd have to remember to be angry with him later. What if pregnant Emma had taken a cupful, thinking it was only coffee?

Scott returned and handed Alexandra a large piece of pie. "You know, you ought to make Joe load the hay wagons all by himself for a week after this," she said.

Scott's fingers brushed hers as he gave her the plate, and she nearly jumped back as if he had burned her. She watched him closely as he took a bite. It was no longer possible for her to look away from him. Her eyes simply wouldn't obey.

With the tips of her fingers, she pulled a sticky slice of peach out of the crust and raised it to Scott's lips. "Want to rehearse the presentation, Mr. Falconer?"

He tossed aside the sweet piece of fruit. "Ladies and gentleman, I'm very pleased to be here today ..." His words trailed off as he kissed her wrist. "I want to make sure of something," he whispered against her bare arm.

"Hmm," she answered dreamily.

He stopped and suddenly grew serious. "I want to make sure that after the presentation is finished and we don't have to focus on it anymore, that we really sit down and talk about us."

"Us?" she asked. "I think that's a good idea. We'll talk then. For real. Talk. Act. Actions speak louder than words, I've heard."

"Are you sure that isn't just Joe's java talking?"

She shook her head once and then nodded it again the other direction. The cobwebs inside just refused to clear somehow. As Scott held her, she smiled, turned around in his arms and drifted off into a peaceful sleep.

"Guess that answers my question."

Scott lifted her in his arms and carried her up the stairs to her room. "You're not making this easy on my back, Alex. This sort of thing looks a whole lot easier in the movies."

She sighed in her sleep—the only response she was capable of giving at that moment. Her thick, auburn hair tumbled across Scott's arm and over her own face. He brushed it back before dropping her gently onto the bed. He removed her shoes, and then thought better of doing what it would take to make her any more comfortable than that. She'd just have to do without those yellow silk pajamas for a night.

•

Alexandra awoke some time past midnight with a vile taste in her mouth. She felt her way along the wall to the bathroom and found some sort of strong, blue mouthwash. Whatever fuel Joe had added to the coffee was nothing short of nauseating—

especially to someone who wasn't naturally a fan of such things in the first place. She smoothed back her hair and started to make her way back to bed when she noticed a faint glow from the living room lights hitting the staircase. Wiping the sleep from her blurry eyes, she started down the steps.

"Scott?" she called out. It was much too late for him to still be awake and too early for him to already be up. They had a flight to catch in just a few hours after all. But who else could possibly be there? She imagined a group of bank robbers straight out of the Old West taking over the main house to hide from the sheriff's posse. It seemed like the right setting for a good western pillage and plunder. How much of that special coffee was still in her bloodstream? she wondered.

"It's me. Just finishing up some work," he yelled back.

"What are you doing up so late?" she asked with a breath of relief and walked the rest of the way downstairs.

Scott looked up from a pile of papers he'd scattered across the top of the coffee table. The television was on with its volume turned down low so as not to wake her, she presumed. "I wanted to go over the presentation numbers one more time, and I had some ranch things to look over after that," he explained. "Did you sleep some of that out of your system?"

"I think so. I'd like to get my hands around your brother's neck, though."

"Join the club."

She sat down beside him and picked up his stack of presentation notes. "I want to thank you for not taking advantage of me a couple hours ago."

"Me? Take advantage of you? Nah."

"You're lucky. I would have had to hurl boxes of take-out food at your head." She knew her mental clarity was returning, because her self-restraint and oddly enough, her old memories had come spinning back.

"Is that your weapon of choice?"

"Weapon of convenience was more like it." She laughed. "Remember that scar on Duncan's forehead?"

His sapphire eyes sparkled. "Somehow, I'm not surprised. I seem to recall a pillow flying my way. And snowballs." He picked up one of his cowboy boots. I figure since we're having our own private slumber party, I might as well get something done. And my boots need oiled badly."

Alexandra grabbed the other boot and a rag. "We really are going to talk after the presentation, aren't we?"

"I don't think we have a choice. I know you're trying to hold me off because we work together. But, Alex, I'd quit my job at D. W. Songstram and work full-time building the dude ranch next month if it would make you take me seriously."

"I take you seriously, Scott. I do. I also know you're probably not looking to get serious with me right after the presentation. That these things take time. You have a lot to deal with."

"You know this for a fact, do you?" he said with great amusement showing on his face. She was conveniently leaving out the cabin, the supply closet ... Not to mention that he'd wanted to marry and spend his life with the right woman so much that he'd almost rushed into a mistake with the wrong one.

"I'm not explaining this right," she said. "I think some of Joe's coffee concoction is still swimming around in my brain. And that's exactly why we shouldn't talk about this subject any more tonight."

"Let's talk in hypothetical generalities, then." He sat the boot in front of the fireplace to let the oil soak in for a while. "Describe your idea of the perfect man. What would he look like, first?"

"Okay. Well, he'd look something like you. But don't attach any great meaning to that."

"Of course not." He couldn't stop smiling for some reason. "What qualities would he have?"

"He'd definitely have to value family life. He'd have good business sense, but good common sense, too. Obviously, he'd have to think I'm the most stunning woman in the universe." She laughed and set down the boot she'd been working on.

"He'd want to grow old together and he'd ooze honor, integrity, loyalty, fidelity. A sense of humor wouldn't hurt if he's going to be around me. Oh, and patience. Lots and lots of patience."

"Haven't thought this through a bit, have you?"

She ignored him. "What about you?"

"She'd be about five feet, nine inches tall. She'd have a stunning wit, a body to die for, auburn hair, green eyes ..."

"Careful, Scott," she warned.

"Look at Miss Conceited thinking she's stunning and irresistible. We're talking in generalities, remember?"

Alexandra blushed furiously. She hated that he could make her do that. "You set me up."

"And it was easy, too. Forget the part about stunning wit. I guess I can do without that."

Alexandra grabbed a pillow and threw it at him. When he ducked she said, "And I guess I can add fast reflexes to my wish list."

He finished laughing and said with all sincerity, "Can I ask a really personal question, Alex?"

"Not a random question? I'm not sure I'll answer it, but you can try."

"That's fair. I want to know why you've made everyone you do business with think you're invincible."

She looked straight into his eyes. "Because that's all that got me through. I could have slinked away with my tail between my legs after what Duncan did to me, or I could make it look like I'd only emerged stronger. I couldn't let anyone see a lapse in judgment. I couldn't let them see a chink in the armor. It's just me in the world, Scott. I don't have any living family. Mary comes the closest. When you're fending for yourself, you tend to put up walls."

Scott nodded. "But don't you know why those people at the Rio Safari gala flocked to you? That had nothing to do with your putting up a front. The business world thinks you're amazing. All the men in that room thought you were amazing, business or no."

"That's the second professional compliment you've given me."

"And are you going to accept this one?"

"I'll think about it." She paused and picked up his boot again. "After the presentation."

Scott got up from the floor and stood with his back to the fireplace. "I've almost got the draft business plan for the dude ranch finished."

"That's wonderful," she said. Her mind still reeled from the way she could have such a personal conversation with him and have it feel so natural.

He crossed his arms over his chest. "What do you really think of the dude ranch idea? Would you do anything with the rest of the land?" This was the test, he thought. He had suddenly been overwhelmed with the need to know how Alexandra Hunter would answer such a question.

She didn't hesitate. "As I said before, I think the idea is brilliant. But I wouldn't touch the rest of the ranch. I mean, I wouldn't develop it or add anything to it just to satisfy guests. You'd kill the atmosphere of the place, I think. Your guests are going to want the closest thing to a real ranch experience they can get. And forgetting about the guests for a minute, you have something really special here, Scott. Something you can keep in the family for generations. You don't know how rare that is. You don't know how rare just having generations of family is!"

Scott hadn't realized he'd been holding his breath awaiting her response. She understood him and the ranch. He suspected if he'd asked the same question of Mackenzie, she would have instantly whipped out sets of blueprints for a Western-themed amusement part. Alexandra was so much the polar opposite of Mackenzie that Scott wanted to reach out, grab her up in his arms, swing her around ...

The dreamy look on his face gave away his changed stream of thought and Alexandra shot him a wide-eyed look of concern. "Are you feeling okay?"

He smiled with that sexy, sweet, lopsided grin of his. "I've never felt better. Really and truly. The world seems just about perfect tonight. But we'd better get some sleep while we can. It's a long trip back to D. W. Songstram."

"But it's not that long until our presentation," Alexandra called down from the stairway. She paused on the steps and watched Scott pile his paperwork into a briefcase. She knew he'd be upstairs as soon as he straightened up the mess he'd made in his father's living room. Now that she'd admitted her feelings to herself and promised to talk to Scott about having a relationship, the anticipation of after the presentation bubbled over in her. For once, she had more than a career victory to look forward to. She had her heart on the line. If this feeling was coffee-related, she hoped it would never wear off.

"We're in the home stretch," he whispered to himself. "Sweet dreams, Alex."

Chapter Eleven

The day of their big presentation to Rio Safari had arrived at long last. Alexandra sat in her office and let the sensations she'd felt with Scott in Montana rush over her. She could scarcely believe how her life had changed since the morning she'd been so angry with David for forcing her to share her project. She smiled to herself. David didn't know he'd given her a blessing in disguise that day he'd let Scott Falconer into her project. He'd given her a cowboy in disguise, too.

After the few days she'd spent with Scott on his family's ranch, Alexandra's heart overflowed with love and longing for the man. She knew without question he desired her, but did his feelings tip over into love? After all their time together, she couldn't imagine anything that could make her doubt him again. She wasn't sure if she was more nervous about the presentation or the discussion she knew they would have after it.

Alexandra pinned her hair up in the most sophisticated style she could arrange and smoothed the wrinkles out of her sharp, black suit. If all went well, she would secure the biggest contract of her career and the greatest love of her life all in one day. She drew in a shaky breath of anticipation and excitement.

As Alexandra drove toward Rio Safari headquarters, she didn't even care if she'd have to face Duncan Phelps and Mac Stevens. They seemed insignificant compared to the emotion running through her. All she could imagine were Scott's laughing blue eyes, his strong hands, his kind smile …

•

Scott arrived early outside the locked conference room doors at Rio Safari. He'd gone over the materials one final time that morning with a feeling of joy. Whether Alexandra was allowed into the room with him or not, he would have her support and that special flair of hers with every slide and every line he spoke.

He was somewhat troubled by the expression he'd seen in David's eyes when he had handed him the list of real estate research they had gathered in Montana. Scott had the keen sense David was hiding more than he was letting on about the purpose behind that trip and the presentation itself. Were the two connected?

Scott had never told Alexandra the extent of Mackenzie's deception while they were dating. If Mac's business tactics ran true to form, he was developing an inkling about what David had stumbled upon. He hoped Alexandra would arrive early enough for him to share his suspicions with her before the presentation.

"Hello, darling." The familiar, sugarcoated voice pulled him out of his thoughts. The platinum blond with her too-red lipstick sauntered over to him and placed her hand on his arm as if they were the closest of friends.

"Mackenzie." He nodded, happy to leave the conversation at a simple greeting.

"I'm so glad I ran into you before the others got here. I wanted to give you a little insider advice before going into that great big room."

Scott removed her hand from his arm. "I don't want any 'advice' that isn't given to the other team, too. You know the rules."

"You hurt my feelings, darling. But I'm going to tell you anyway."

"With your take on business ethics, I'm somehow not surprised." He tried to walk away, but Mac stepped in front of him, posing to emphasize her prized curves.

"Scott Falconer," she purred, "there's only one way D. W.

Songstram is going to win this contract, and believe me, it has nothing to do with the dog and pony show you put on in there."

Scott felt anger rising and tightening in his chest. "What are you saying, Mac? That you've rigged the whole thing? Because if that's what you're admitting ..."

Mac wiggled a step closer, uncomfortably invading his space. "No, silly. There's nothing that sinister to admit. It's just that the rest of the board of directors and I have been talking. No matter how good your numbers are on this project, what we really need is customer service first and foremost."

Scott wasn't following her and wanted to end the conversation. "Then our approach will go over very well with all of you. Excuse me." He gently moved her aside and took a step away when her voice stopped him again.

"You're not understanding me." She narrowed her cat-like eyes, knowing she finally had his attention. "You see, we want personalized care. We want someone on site—one of your team located right there in Rio Safari's office."

Her meaning slowly sunk in on him. Her argument made no sense for this project. What Mac Stevens wanted was either Duncan Phelps or himself seated in an office next to hers. Business was obviously the farthest thing from her self-indulgent, spoiled mind.

"I won't be anyone's puppet, Mackenzie. And you have some nerve even suggesting it."

•

Alexandra walked briskly down the empty hall, shoes sinking softly into the short, cushiony carpeting. She'd seen Scott's car parked in the lot outside, and couldn't wait to see him before the review panel and the competition arrived. It was hard to go even a day without hearing his voice, seeing his face ...

As she neared the corner, the hum of heated whispers reached her ears. She leaned quietly against the wall and slowly peeked around the corner. The first thing she saw was Mackenzie Stevens with her exaggerated posture leaning toward Scott. Decked out in a scarlet red suit, Mac's aggressive body language was enough to make Alexandra want to rip the woman's white-blond hair out. Alexandra almost revealed herself when it looked like Scott could use some help. But then Mackenzie's next words drifted toward her.

"Scott, my darling. It all boils down to this. You need to change your presentation and fast. If we don't hear that you're committing to relocate to my office, you won't win. It's that simple. I want you at my disposal, day and night. If I don't hear you making yourself available to my—to Rio Safari's needs, the contract goes to Duncan. I think we can bring new meaning to 'it's a pleasure doing business with you,' if you know what I mean."

Alexandra couldn't believe she had heard the words she'd just heard. Was Mac Stevens for real? She was still seething when she heard muffled footsteps coming toward her. She composed herself quickly and pretended she had just come from the restroom.

Duncan walked past her with a smug, contemptible look on his face. "Eavesdropping, Ms. Hunter? How unladylike."

"Drop dead," she hissed at Duncan with a plastic smile affixed to her face. With the rest of the Zellez team and Rio Safari executives close behind, she walked over and stood beside Scott.

•

"I'm sure glad to see you," he whispered to her. He was stunned at the interaction he had just had with Mac. The woman was even more tactless, brazen and despicable than he'd remembered. Next to Alexandra, she looked like a cheap imitation of corporate class. Did she actually think he'd prostitute himself and lose Alexandra just to win a contract? Alexandra meant more to him than all the millions in the world. Especially after their visit to the ranch, nothing could change that for him.

Mac unlocked the conference room doors and interrupted the greetings in the hall. It was clear to Scott that she wanted to prevent him from having a chance to confer with his partner before the presentation. He wouldn't have expected anything lower from her.

"Gentlemen," Mac said, "if the Zellez team representative could step inside and go on back to the private waiting room. The D. W. Songstram presenter can go ahead and set up."

Scott touched Alexandra's shoulder lightly. "Sorry, Alex. I wish we could talk, but apparently, duty calls."

Duncan and Scott stepped inside and Mac clicked the heavy double-doors shut behind them, not missing the chance to give Alex a look of unmasked hostility. Clearly the woman thought she'd beaten her at some self-imagined game.

Alexandra sat in the hall with Roger and Mike chatting about small things with them for the first time since the Rio Safari holiday gala. They smiled and nodded, vying for her attention, though she didn't notice.

Alexandra's thoughts were divided between her present conversation and the one she'd just heard, and an insecure fear slowly crept over her. Scott wouldn't cave to Mac's sleazy demands, would he? This contract was worth millions. The glow of happiness she'd felt only minutes before began to dim. Just imagine what his share of the bonus could do for the family ranch. How much was that worth to him?

She was ashamed of herself. The strong, honest man she'd come to know would never stoop to such a level. She had to stop doubting him at every turn. They would lose the contract, but walk away with their integrity. But, what if … ? That first drop of uncertainty was insidious. She'd promised Scott when they were locked in the supply closet that if she ever started to doubt him, she would wait. She'd give him a chance without jumping to conclusions. When Rio Safari announced Zellez as the winner of the contract, all her questions would be answered, her fears wiped away.

An hour passed and then another while they waited in the hall. Roger snored quietly in the corner and Mike reread the newspaper. Finally, the door clicked open and one of the board members poked his head out into the hall.

"We're falling way behind schedule in here. We're not going to need you folks inside later for the questions, so feel free to leave. I can't give you any idea how long this is going to take."

Mike nudged Roger awake. "Sounds like we're being politely dismissed."

Alexandra couldn't believe what she'd just heard. "So it seems." What could possibly be happening behind those locked doors? Frustrated, she drove back to the office.

When she arrived, Sarah's curiosity was visibly getting the better of her. "Well?" she asked, "what happened?"

"Can you believe they still have Scott in there? The presentations ran over and they told the rest of us to leave."

"Ouch." Sarah followed Alexandra into her office. "David has been by here a dozen times this morning. Guess he wanted to talk to you pretty badly. I wouldn't worry, though. With Scott and Mac Stevens so close and all, I can't imagine we'll lose this one."

Alexandra turned around slowly to face her assistant. "What exactly do you mean by 'close'?"

There was no way Sarah could miss the look on her boss' face. She was on shaky ground. "Well, you know that day you were out with food poisoning?"

Alexandra remembered it well. That was the day Scott had found the fax from Rio Safari, the fax that had eliminated her from her own presentation. She nodded.

"I overheard him calling up Ms. Stevens," she stammered nervously as Alexandra's expression grew darker. "Actually, he had me get her on the line for him. I just overheard him saying how much he needed to see her."

"Could you have interpreted it wrong?" Alexandra asked. The lingering doubt from earlier that morning threatened to take over her common sense.

"I don't know. He shut the door like it was a private conversation, though."

Alexandra shook her head. She'd been down this road before, and it never led to the right conclusion. "Sarah, I'm tired of the gossip. I really am. I was wrong to ask you and I won't do it again. Now could you close my door on the way out? Unless it's David, I don't want to see anyone."

Alexandra covered her face with her hands and moaned.

"Nerves?" David's familiar voice came from behind the door.

"Come on in, David. I'm just waiting. And putting an end to my own stupidity once and for all." She smoothed her hair back and smiled at him. "What's up? I hear you've been by a few times."

David sat down and grinned at her. "When Scott gets back, I have a lot to tell the two of you."

"So mysterious, David? Must be juicy."

"Oh, it is. Very juicy. But not as tantalizing as the news I just got a minute ago."

Alexandra scooted to the edge of her seat. "I can't stand the drama," she said.

David leaned forward and whispered. "We just won the Rio Safari contract."

Alexandra's heart plummeted then soared. Should she laugh, cry, scream?

David stared at his vice president in confusion. "Aren't you going to say anything?"

"Congratulations, David. This will be very good for the company." She opened her mouth to say more and then snapped it shut.

"There's more? I hope there's more because that wasn't the happy reaction I expected."

"Here's what bothers me, David. I heard Mac tell Scott there was no way we'd win unless he—"

"Oh. Yes, I get the picture. But I don't think that's why we won."

For the first time, none of her insecurities surfaced. She smiled broadly. "You know, I don't think so either. Scott isn't like that. Ha! Can you believe it? I *know* he isn't like that. And I know this comes out of the blue, but I'd like to take the next few days off, David. Would that be all right?"

She heard David hesitantly agree to her request for time off before she grabbed up her purse and walked briskly from her office. Life looked bright. Very bright. She felt the weight of the world lift from her shoulders.

"Life is good." She waved as she walked away.

"But I need to talk to you later," David called after her.

"I'll be back." The Terminator himself couldn't have said it better.

She'd just helped earn the biggest contract of her career. She'd just been part of D. W. Songstram's biggest team presentation ever. And then there was Scott ...

•

When Scott returned and learned Alexandra had gone without an explanation, David suffered another strange reaction from him. His executives had either gone insane or fallen in love with each other somewhere along the way, that much was obvious. In fact, he had begun to suspect the latter some while ago. David thought back to when he and his wife had first met and recalled that there wasn't much difference between those two conditions.

When Scott had muttered something to him about Mac Steven's last-minute demand, the pieces fell into place.

"She didn't believe you'd stoop to that demand for a minute, Falconer."

Scott nodded. "Then we've come farther than you can imagine. Wow. Just—wow."

David put his hand on the younger man's shoulder. "Far be it from me to interfere in your personal life. But from what I can tell, there's sometimes been a breakdown in communication between you and Alexandra. Go to her and celebrate everything that happened today. She doesn't have all the details yet and I'm sure she'd love to hear them from you. She also asked for a few days off. She's never done that before. Just thought you should know."

"I think I could use a few days off myself."

"Fine. I'm getting soft in my old age, but I think you've earned it."

As Scott's footsteps disappeared down the hall, David's eyes lit up with an idea and he picked up his phone. His wife, Connie, wouldn't believe what he was about to do, but he wouldn't miss this moment for the world.

Chapter Twelve

She'd barely returned home from work when she heard the voicemail from David asking her to meet him in the lobby of their building. As she'd seen him only an hour before, she couldn't imagine why he wanted her there again so soon. He promised in the message their meeting wouldn't take long, but even a few minutes at the office seemed like too many for her. Her phone showed another missed call from Scott. She just wanted to call him, go shopping, have dinner, start a life that involved something other than the inside of that building ...

When she looked in the mirror, the face staring back at her seemed the same as it always did. Only Alexandra knew it was a public image constructed very carefully over the years. But upon closer inspection, now that image looked happy. She fairly glowed. She'd never loved anyone the way she did Scott. She remembered the touch of his hand as they danced under the stars. Her heart almost hurt as she thought of the slight wave of his dark hair, rumpled from fingers run through it too many times while working numbers.

Just as she was headed back toward her car, Mary came over with coffee and muffins to lend her moral support—just in case the presentation had gone badly. "Well?"

"We won! And I think Scott might— I think *I* might ..."

"Aw. My little girl is growing up."

"We're the same age, Mary." She rolled her eyes.

"But I have you outweighed in experience."

"So should I go for it?"

Mary shook her head. "Duh. You've got it bad for this guy, and with good reason. Let me put this into perspective. He's a family man who's amazing to look at, good with cars, crunches numbers and feeds cattle—think you'll find that combination again? He just slips right back and forth between two worlds effortlessly. He's amazing."

Oh, she needed to find Scott and she needed to find him now. David sure had timing, didn't he?

"Go, Alex. Live a little. Get out of here!"

She laughed as she drove past the place on the freeway where she'd had the flat tire and Scott had come to her rescue. He'd caught her attention even then. When Mary was right, she was really right. Alexandra took out her phone and dialed Scott. Straight to voicemail. She tried the office.

"Hi, it's Alexandra. Can you put me through to Scott Falconer?"

The receptionist put her on hold for what seemed an eternity before coming back onto the line. "Sorry," she said. "Mr. Falconer isn't here right now. You might try again later."

Alexandra hung up. "Great," she said to herself as she pulled her car into the lot. Just as she neared the elevators, David rounded the corner in time to meet her. He almost knocked a leafy green plant off its decorative stand in the process, and quickly caught it.

"Punctual as always," he said with a wide, nervous-looking smile.

"Did I forget to sign something?" Alexandra asked.

David certainly didn't seem his usual self. Was he fidgeting? She hoped he wasn't angry with her for leaving so abruptly.

"I'll explain why I asked you to come here in the elevator on the way up." David pushed the button and, always the gentleman, held his hand on the door for Alexandra to enter first.

To say she was startled when he didn't get in behind her and the doors shut would be an understatement.

•

Several floors up and several minutes earlier, Scott had waited outside the elevator for a signal.

David's cryptic message had lured him back to the office and he still wasn't sure why. As he'd stepped off the elevator into the reception area just a few minutes before, David had literally run out to greet him. He'd shoved a dozen long-stem red roses, a box of truffles and a bottle of champagne into Scott's arms and told him to wait there.

Then his boss had gotten into the elevator, said something about needing to test it, and instructed him to ride it down to the ground floor lobby when David sent it back up for him.

Was that sweat he'd seen glistening on David's forehead? When the elevator doors opened again, inside the elevator was the one person on earth he'd been dying to see.

"Scott," Alex gasped.

Scott stepped inside and the doors shut a bit too quickly behind him. He jumped. "That's not normal."

"I know." Alexandra violently punched the button to open the door.

"Trapped alone with me again, are you? Seems to be a trend." Scott whispered.

She pushed each button one at a time with newfound enthusiasm, but none of them lit up. Suddenly the elevator lurched, carried them several flights higher, and then stopped with a jolt. She pulled open the little stainless steel panel to the emergency telephone and found a bunch of wires leading to nothing. Someone had obviously removed the phone so that they couldn't even call out for help, and she had a good idea who the culprit was.

"Don't worry," Scott said. "David is well aware we're stuck here. He's a tricky one."

David's voice came over the speaker. "I want you two to communicate. You have thirty minutes to do nothing but talk, and I suggest you use them all. I'll turn off the camera so you have some privacy."

"David, there's no need to matchmake. I think we have it

figured out this time," Alex said.

"What about the speaker?" Scott asked.

David sighed. "Sure. I'll turn it off to. Thirty minutes, kids." His voice cracked and the speaker went dead.

Scott sighed. "I think I have a lot to tell you. At least David thinks so." Then he chuckled. "He forgot to take away our cell phones."

"At any rate, I'm listening." Alexandra's pulse began to race again. She kicked off her shoes and sank down to the floor to await rescue. "I already know we won. Why did we win, Scott? I heard Mac and I know you wouldn't go back to her. So, how?"

Scott sat down on the floor of the elevator beside her and handed her the roses.

"They're gorgeous." She smiled. "Give me the chocolates."

"I never told you what Mac tried to do when we were involved. I was younger and stupider at the time, and she seemed to attract a lot of attention. I guess I figured there must be so much buzz around her for a reason and I wanted to find out what it was."

"I don't need to know everything," Alex said.

"You do. Because I think we have a chance here, and I don't want any skeletons falling out of the closet later on. Anyway, she didn't even pay attention to me at first. She hung out with local politicians and businessmen with high enough titles. But all of the sudden, one day she called me and asked me out to dinner. I thought she was interested in my life—in me.

"Mac couldn't seem to ask enough questions about my family and the ranch. My parents had been so happy together there. I wanted that same happiness with my own wife one day. I was thrilled that Mac would care about these things."

Alexandra nodded. "But she didn't?"

"Oh, she was interested in the ranch all right. Just not for the reasons I thought. I couldn't have paid her enough to go ice-skating on the ditch, much less get within a hundred yards of a mud puddle or a cow.

"As it turned out, she was busy assessing our operations

and looking for our fatal flaw. She was systematically picking out our financial weaknesses. Cattle disappeared by the dozen. Fences would be mysteriously cut down in the night. Our alfalfa fields turned brown and died out no matter what we did. We finally had some samples tested and knew for sure someone had sprayed a mix of chemicals on them, but we had no idea who could have done it. All the while I kept turning to and confiding in Mac, the woman I thought I loved, for comfort.

"After a few months of this, Dad was on the verge of putting the whole place up for sale and moving to Florida. That's when the offer came in—completely out of the blue—from a retired banker in the area. The offer was so low we thought it was a joke at first. But, as we lost more and more money, Dad started to actually consider it."

The tiny stress line appeared on Alexandra's face. "You could have been ruined. How on earth did you guys save the ranch with all that happening?"

"By sheer accident. I drove into Helena one day, quite unplanned. I hadn't even told Mac about my daytrip because I was considering shopping for an engagement ring, if you can believe that. Shopping, mind you, not buying yet.

"Anyway, as I was driving past a little roadside hotel, I saw the same man who had just made the pathetic offer on the ranch walking out of his room. It seemed a little off to me that a man of such wealth was hanging around a dirty hotel in the middle of the day. I pulled the car over to talk to him, and that's when I looked through the open door and saw Mac sitting on the edge of the bed getting dressed."

Alexandra's hand flew to her mouth in horror. "She'd set the whole thing up."

Scott nodded grimly. "She saw land and pictured dollar signs. Seems she wanted to build a resort there—like she did with those ski cabins in Colorado. I was just a means to an end."

"So what happened?"

A twinkle came back into Scott's eyes. "I pulled the car away from the hotel before they saw me, and we played it cool for a while. My father actually followed the retired banker around with a camera for a few days. He got some very interesting pictures, which he threatened to give to the man's wife and every political committee he belonged to. Dad walked away with a check for all the damages to the ranch and then some that day."

Alexandra smiled and placed her hand over Scott's. "I'm sorry. If I'd known what Mac did, I don't think I would ever have thought what I thought when you got that fax—not for a second. I still don't understand how our presentation won, though. I don't understand why you knowing her would be a benefit to our team, for that matter."

"Because she wasn't the only person I knew at Rio, Alex. There are a lot of good people there and I hoped they would cancel out her influence."

"So how did we win, considering she was so bent on getting you back?"

"I was just getting to that," Scott said. "I went in there and gave the presentation exactly as we'd rehearsed it, Alex. I didn't change a thing. You should have seen her face. She was *livid*."

Alexandra would have enjoyed the satisfaction of watching Mac's reaction in person. "I can just imagine."

Scott laughed. "I thought I'd blown it for sure. And then one of the review panel members got a call on his cell phone. I don't know what happened after that—it was nuts. The entire panel excused itself and went back to the waiting room with Duncan."

"That's probably when things got drawn out and they told me and the other guys to leave," Alexandra added.

"I think it was. They were in there at least an hour before they came out and asked me to leave as well. I passed the police in the hallway on my way out."

"The police?" Alexandra was intrigued. "Really?"

"This is where David filled things in for me. He was the one who'd called that board member on his cell phone. Apparently, all those company names we brought back from Montana were dummy corporations."

Alexandra knew what had to be coming next. "You don't mean Mac Stevens was behind them all?"

Scott smiled as if he'd scored a long-overdue victory. "When Rio Safari became interested in a property, her dummy corporation would buy it up. Of course, she was in charge of all the real estate purchases for Rio. She would fake negotiations and basically write out an exorbitant check to herself from Rio funds."

"Unbelievable," Alexandra gasped.

"Just wait. It gets better," he teased, holding her gaze until an unspoken meaning reached her.

"Duncan was in on it somehow. Probably getting some kind of under-the-table payoff," she almost yelled. "And they both were caught."

Scott beamed. "Ain't it grand? Mac fired and jailed in one fell swoop."

"And Duncan finally gets what's coming to him," Alexandra squealed. "Do you think they'll look into his past? Into all the things he stole from me and my last company?"

"They already are," Scott whispered.

Tears brimmed in Alexandra's eyes. After so many years, justice had finally triumphed. "Tell me what happened when the police got there. I want details."

He reached out and delicately wiped a tear away from Alexandra's nose. "I waited in the hall to see what was going to happen. It was the most satisfying moment I've ever witnessed. They even put handcuffs on both of them. Mac kept saying things like 'Do you know who I am?' It was hysterical. I actually thought the front of her jacket was going to rip open when they pulled her hands behind her back. You know how tight her clothes always fit."

"I can picture it now. What about Duncan and his stupid, ugly, stupid beard?"

"He kept saying something about you setting him up. Then Mac yelled at him to shut up because he was caught and ought to be smart enough to know it. Then he accused *her* of setting him up. He got really quiet and started picking lint off his tweed jacket and smoothing his beard until one of the officers clamped the cuffs on him."

Alexandra closed her eyes and reveled in the scene he'd described for her. "I'm so sorry I ever doubted you," she finally said. "I never should have. I almost did again, but I caught myself."

Scott put his head in his hands. "Not the fabulously accurate Sarah again?"

"She heard you telling Mac you needed her that day I was out sick."

Scott shook his head. "She heard me telling Mac how sleazy I thought that fax was. I was trying to get you back in place as the presenter." He ran his thumb gently across her cheekbone, pulled her close and held her. "Do you realize this is the 'after the presentation' time we talked about?"

Alexandra gazed up into his eyes. "It is, isn't it?"

"You know what else I realize?"

She shook her head. "What?"

"That I would have rather lost millions of dollars than lose you."

His lips brushed hers. It had been too many days since he'd held her, kissed her. He wanted to tell her how much he'd come to love her, wanted to show her in every way he knew how.

Suddenly, they felt another jolt and to their disappointment, the elevator began to move. Before the doors opened, Alexandra gazed up at Scott with eyes just a little mistier than she'd meant to allow.

He looked down at her lovely face and whispered, "I'm in love with you, Alexandra Hunter."

"I know," she whispered back, and with a wicked grin, jumped out of the elevator.

"Oh, come on," Scott called out as he chased after her. He shrugged at a very entertained David as Alexandra scooted out the door and headed across the lobby toward the parking lot.

Scott caught up with her just before the front doors and

found her laughing in near hysteria. "I'm just so relieved," she said.

Scott gathered her into his arms. "You're such a pill. A man professes his undying love for a woman and gets nothing in return. Not a word?"

"Don't worry, Falconer. I have the impression you usually get what you want."

"I'm not so sure."

Then she wrapped her arms around his neck and whispered, "I love you."

"Random question," he whispered back. Then he quietly dropped to one knee and pulled a small velvet box from his pocket.

Epilogue

With snowflakes sticking to the windows and a roaring fire lighting up the room, Scott and Alexandra celebrated their wedding at the family ranch and immediately drove away to begin their honeymoon. The night seemed like the fulfillment of a long-awaited dream.

Alexandra gazed into Scott's eyes with an anxious excitement that surprised her. She had long since given up the illusion of composure around him. The combination of rancher and businessman she had found in him assured her that her life with him would never be a dull one. Even the faintest brush of his hand sent shudders through her. She loved watching him work at the ranch—and she loved seeing him in a suit with his briefcase in hand. A woman couldn't ask for a better husband, she thought.

Scott carried Alexandra through the doorway to the most expensive honeymoon suite he could find in Helena. "I guess I really will get to see Paris in a couple days," he said while thinking of their final honeymoon destination. "You'll have to tell me what kinds of adventures Sarah claims I've had there. We'll make all those rumors true together."

Alexandra grinned. "Why, Mr. Falconer, are you coming on to me?"

"I wouldn't dare. You know how these office romances always turn out."

Alexandra looked around the suite and saw it had been

prepared with lighted candles and flower petals. Sitting on the nightstand, she spotted a small wooden box. She slid out of Scott's arms and walked over to it.

"Is this the box I admired at the holiday festival we went to?"

Scott smiled softly. "Look inside."

She opened the box and pulled out a small, plastic card. "What's this?" She laughed and flipped it over in her hand.

He walked over to her. "The number for roadside assistance in Montana."

Alexandra put her arms around him. "Good idea for a present." She nuzzled against him. "I tend to meet the most attractive men whenever I get a flat tire."

Scott ran his hand through Alexandra's thick hair and pulled her head back gently. How was it that this stunning woman had agreed to spend the rest of her life with him? He planned to live up to that honor if it took the remainder of his years.

Her green eyes and his blue ones shone like gemstones in the candlelit room as their gazes locked.

"I don't think corporate rank counts here, do you?" she teased.

"Not at all," was the last thing she remembered him say in that moment.

Days later, Scott and Alexandra returned to the headquarters of D. W. Songstram with a plan in mind. Even before their trip to Paris, they agreed that Montana would become home for them. Scott knew the time for him to start his own business venture had come at last. With Alexandra at his side, he wanted more than anything to build his guest ranch on the property he and his brother, Elliot, had just purchased.

Scott and Alexandra sat in David's office, waiting intently as he thought in silence for a moment. David tapped the tips of his fingers together for a long while and hunkered down in his chair.

"I hate to lose you both," he said with a misty, sentimental look in his eyes. He fancied himself at least partially responsible for Scott and Alexandra finally finding each other. Even his wife told everyone David had turned into a halfway decent matchmaker.

Scott smiled sadly, "But you understand why we have to do this? If there was any way one of us could stay and work for you, we would. It's just that living in Montana would make for one heck of a commute."

"Then let me run something by you two," David said as he reached for a heavy file behind him. "Alexandra, this may be something you'd be interested in."

"You definitely have my attention." She hoped David had something up his sleeve. He often did.

"Well," David said with a look of mischief, "after you brought back all that property information from Montana and we blew the lid off of that scam, Rio Safari won't touch some of that property they once wanted to buy. There's an office building in Helena that's just gone into foreclosure—with Mac Stevens in jail not making payments and all. I put in a bid to the bank and it was accepted today."

Alexandra looked from Scott to David. "So you're opening an office there?"

"Honestly, I've been looking at doing just that for quite some time. What I need is a class act with enough corporate expertise to move to Montana and run the place." He looked at his vice president in anticipation.

"You mean me?" she asked as her heart started to pound with excitement. She couldn't ask for more. In one sublime stroke of fate, her career and love life had reached epic proportions. She suddenly couldn't wait to call and talk to Mary. She wouldn't believe it, either. She'd probably want to move to Montana, too.

Scott took her hand when she didn't answer immediately, mistaking her pause for hesitation. "Think about it. While Elliot and I are up to our eyeballs in construction and cow manure ..."

Alexandra shook her head and laughed. "No need to sell me on it. I'm convinced already. It's the perfect offer, David. Thank you. Oh, and I'll give you a call later to talk about that raise I just know you have in mind."

David winced. After all, he knew that determined look of hers. He looked at Scott. "Ask the receptionist to screen my calls on the way out, will you?"

Alexandra smiled brightly and her heels clicked on the familiar tiled floor as she walked out of David's office with her husband right by her side. They had a lot of packing to do, but it would have to wait. As they passed the supply closet, Scott grabbed Alexandra by the arm and pulled her inside.

He nuzzled her neck as she sat down on that stack of boxes she had come to know so well. "All right, Falconer. I sense grounds for a sexual harassment lawsuit coming on."

He murmured against her, "I'd better make this worth all the dire legal repercussions—" He placed a sweet kiss on her mouth. "—and make this good enough that at least one person in the world will be happy with me today."

Her former words came back to her. "Rest assured, Scott Falconer—I'm extremely happy."

• • •

A Wife by Accident

She wasn't looking for trouble,
which is why she ran smack into it.

VICTORIA ASHE

**She wasn't looking for trouble,
which is why she ran smack into it.**

Hayely Black has cut herself off from her wealthy parents, determined to make it on her own. Then one misstep leads her into more than one kind of crunch. Stuck in a dead-end job and now indebted to Nevada's most eligible bachelor, Hayely agrees to an arrangement she never would have considered before.

Gary Tarleton, self-made bazillionaire, has lived with the secrets of his past all his adult life, and within those secrets is a childhood dream all the money in the world can't fulfill. As he looks at charming Hayely, he sees the answer to a prayer—and the possibility of the kind of family he thought he'd never have.